COAL

BOOK ONE OF THE EVERLEAF SERIES

DEDICATION

"Write the book you want to read"—*Toni Morrison*

These people not only made writing less lonely for me, but they made *Coal* better: Heather L, Becky, Tahmeka, Christina, Sara. And of course, my Wattpad crew: dostwinjas, greyrabit75, Lomber09, and brownstickybunz. Thanks for giving me the confidence I needed to publish.

I also want to give a special thanks to my husband and my kids for giving me permission to take the time I needed to pursue my dreams.

CONTENTS

CHAPTER ONE

Coal held the newly forged sword at arm's length. The sentient weapon vibrated in his grasp, urging him to attack, but he tightened his sweaty hands around the leather hilt and ignored the foreign impulses. He had been forging swords and practicing with the completed weapons long enough to know when to attack and when to bide his time and let the fight come to him.

Grigory, the master swordsmith, advanced. Coal parried, stepping aside and swinging his sword with all of the skill he'd gained from the two years of working the forge. Grigory fell to the ground, effortlessly rolling beneath the sword before bouncing back to his feet.

"Is she overwhelming you?" Grigory asked as they faced each other. They had been dueling for the past hour. Sweat dripped from Coal's forehead, back, and arms, but just like every other time they'd dueled, the master swordsmith showed no sign of exertion.

"She's restless." Coal wiped the sweat from his forehead with the back of his hand. "But I'm in contr—"

Grigory rushed forward with an arcing swipe. Coal raised his sword to meet the strike. For a moment, their strengths were equal. His sword vibrated with glee as Coal threatened to overcome Grigory.

Forcing the sword's excitement to the back of his mind, Coal focused all of his strength into his upper body and pushed outward.

Overwhelmed, Grigory leaped back.

During the two years of forging swords and sparring with the master swordsmith, Coal had never had the strength or skill to complete such a move. For an instant, he let himself—and the sword—enjoy their accomplishment.

He was so distracted by his small victory that he almost didn't notice when Grigory spun around, his left leg heading towards Coal's knees. Coal dove away, Grigory's boots just skimming his leg. He rolled over to find a sword pointed at his neck.

Grigory lowered his blade. "You were distracted."

"I almost had you," Coal said with an intense rush of pride and confidence.

"You did not," Grigory said, scratching the eye patch over his left eye. "You've been slow and lazy all morning."

"But I finally completed the block."

"Not with any speed. You're gaining strength and height, but that's nothing to be proud of. What is the point of winning the bind if you are beheaded a moment later?"

Coal let Grigory's words sink in while he caught his breath. "You're right. I've been a little distracted. I'm supposed to meet Princess Chalcedony soon." He glanced at the sun, trying to gauge the time. It hung low in the morning sky, but the springtime rays were much stronger than they were when he'd arrived.

Time for him to go.

Grigory lifted the eyebrow above his remaining eye. The other had been gouged out 200 years ago when he served as a soldier instead of a swordsmith. "How long has it been since you've seen her?"

Coal bit his lip while he pretended to think about the answer he already knew. "Two months."

Grigory took the sword from Coal's hands. It would be presented to Chalcedony on her coronation as queen. Magic reinforced the silver shaft, and its black leather hilt emanated heat and welcomed touch. By far, it was the best sword they'd forged.

"Before you go, I have something to ask you." Grigory kept his shoulder-length black hair tied in a low ponytail and his beard trimmed. Both elven and dwarf blood coursed through his veins. As the only known half-breed of his kind, he had the height of an elf and the thick, muscular build of a dwarf.

"What is it?" Coal asked. The way Grigory spoke made Coal wonder if he'd done something wrong, besides being too distracted during the fight.

"I'm getting older," Grigory said. "I need to choose a full-time apprentice, and it needs to be soon. Do you want the position?"

Coal's breath caught in his throat. Had he heard right? "I thought I was just helping out until you found a full-time apprentice?"

"Well, you've passed the two-year audition, and now I'm offering you the job."

"But humans can't do magic." It was one of the first things Coal had learned when he'd arrived in the fey realm eleven years ago. Powerful swords were impossible to make without magic. It made the swords stronger, lighter, and prevented someone else from using it.

"I'm half dwarf and half elf," Grigory said. "For years, my master refused to teach me because he didn't think a half-breed could make a great sword. Now, I am the best swordsmith in Everleaf. It's what's inside that makes a good swordsmith. I believe you could be one of the greats."

Coal had been coming to the forge almost every day for two years, but he was allowed to come and go as he pleased. With a full apprenticeship, he'd eat, breathe, and sleep smithing. He'd have to move out of his home.

"I don't know, Grigory. I need time to think about it." Coal enjoyed forging swords. He especially loved practicing with them, ensuring they would endure battle, but he didn't know if he wanted to make it his life's work.

"Your childhood friend is soon to be queen. She will not have time, or tolerance, for a lovesick human."

Coal was hurt, but not surprised by Grigory's words. No one said anything to his face, but he heard the servants and soldiers gossiping about him and Princess Chalcedony when they thought he wasn't listening. "You're right, but give me time. It's not easy choosing one life over another."

Grigory's eye softened. "You and the future queen still have much growing to do. Decide soon. I won't wait long."

Coal glanced back towards the rising sun. "It's time for me to go."

Grigory waved his hand as if to swat a fly, before he turned back to the forge.

Bees and butterflies as big as his hands buzzed around Coal's ankles while he walked through a meadow of red, yellow, and blue wildflowers that separated the forge from his home. He felt guilty for not accepting Grigory's offer, but as he approached his home, the guilt faded and a smile grew across his face. He lived in Legacy, the biggest tree in the fey realm, with his best friend Princess Chalcedony, her staff, and a handful of ambassadors from every part of the realm.

At 850-feet tall and ten times as wide as Grigory's modest home, Legacy seemed to be larger than life. Residing inside of a living, sentient thing, made him feel like he was a part of something remarkable. The moment he saw it years ago, Coal knew he'd made it home.

"Legacy." Coal touched the coarse bark of the oak tree and instantly felt the life thrumming inside it. "Is Chalcedony back?"

There are so many here today. How am I supposed to keep track of any one person? Legacy said, its voice full of annoyance. Legacy was neither male nor female, but its voice sounded female nonetheless.

"Come on, Legacy. Is she in her room?"

The tree gave an exaggerated sigh as the breeze rustled its leaves. *When last I bothered to listen, she was in her office and she was asking for you.*

"Thanks," Coal said, relieved to hear that Princess Chalcedony had returned. He removed his hand and approached the two female sentries guarding Legacy's main entrance. Like all of Everleaf's elven soldiers, they wore a dark green shirt with black sleeves and black pants.

"Where are you going?" asked the taller of the two, who had light green eyes. She stepped in his way, blocking the door. "The servant's entrance is around the back."

"I'm not a servant." Coal held the sentry's gaze. He'd never seen these two before, but he'd done this dance countless times over the years. He was a human in a world where humans were mostly banned and thought of as violent, ignorant, and greedy. His stomach churned as he faced the sentry, but he stood his ground. If he showed fear, it only made the taunting worse.

"No." The other sentry stood a head shorter than her partner, but where the other was slender, she was more muscular. "He's not a servant. He's just human trash."

He swallowed. "Let me through."

"Or what?" The taller sentry placed a hand on her sword. "You'll tell the princess I was picking on you?"

"I don't need the princess to protect me," he snapped. "I can take care of myself."

"Calm down, Sophia," the shorter sentry said. "Let him through. Today will be his last day here anyway."

"What are you talking about?" Coal narrowed his eyes, his pulse quickened. This was not part of the usual bullying.

"Don't worry about it," the sentry said, pulling the green-eyed sentry away from Coal. "I apologize for my partner. Her great-great something or other died in the human and fey wars."

"Well ..." Coal deepened his voice, his attitude bolstered by the change in her tone. "Don't let it happen again."

"Of course not." The shorter sentry bowed. "Again, I apologize."

Coal walked past the sentries and through the entrance, deciding they had only been trying to scare him. But why would she say it was his last day here?

Once he entered the grand hall separating the entranceway from Chalcedony's offices, he understood why Legacy sounded upset. Staff bringing food from the kitchen and filling mugs with milk, juices, and mead crowded the hall with bustling energy. Almost every race of fey had gathered here—or at least every race of fey that ventured out in the daytime—elves, giants, dwarves, satyrs, nymphs, and even a few trolls.

Coal touched the wall and said to Legacy, "The ambassadors aren't supposed to be here until tomorrow." It had been quiet for the past three weeks. However, now that Chalcedony had returned from the human realm, fey from every corner of Everleaf came to meet with her.

Obviously, they decided to come early, Legacy said.

Disappointed, Coal broke the connection with the tree. Before she'd left on her last training trip, Chalcedony had said she had something special planned for the two of them. Her duties came first, though. If she had to work, she wouldn't have time for him.

He peered into the crowd, searching for the path of least resistance. Finding it, he lowered his head, stepped out of the safety of the entranceway, and walked into the congested gathering. The smell of goat sausage and fried eggs wafted towards him, making his stomach rumble with hunger. He'd awakened before the kitchen staff, and only had time to eat an apple before he'd left for Grigory's.

"Did you really think you were going to walk by me without speaking?" A deep voice said from behind. Coal twisted around and looked up into the gray eyes of the eight-foot tall, tawny-skinned giant named Octavius.

"Soon…" Octavius winked one of his gray eyes at Coal, "I hear you'll be reigning next to Chalcedony."

"Princess Chalcedony and I are only friends," Coal answered, suddenly losing his appetite. Humans were considered weak. If Chalcedony took on a human mate, she would be considered weak also.

The day had started full of promise. He'd looked forward to spending time with Chalcedony, but his plans were quickly unraveling. With the giants and dwarves here, it would be impossible for her to slip away. And, for the second time today, someone had reminded him he didn't belong.

"Don't look so insulted." Octavius grabbed Coal's shoulder. "My great-great-grandmother was human. I'd consider it an honor to have a human reigning beside the queenling."

"Hmph, that would never happen," said Ambassador Eli. The dwarf seemed to have appeared out of nowhere, his head a mass of dark curls. "Humans are exiled for a reason. They are violent, greedy, and, above all, parasitic." He stared at Coal with light blue eyes and sneered.

Octavius shook his head and clicked his tongue. "No, giants are humans, only taller. That's why we can't wield magic. And there is nothing extraordinarily violent or parasitic about us."

"Stop it with the myths. That's like saying dwarves are human, only shorter," Ambassador Eli said. "If your brother heard you speak like that, he'd have you whipped."

The temptation to stay and listen to Octavius and Ambassador Eli argue nearly overpowered him, but the idea of seeing Chalcedony pulled much stronger. They were too busy debating the differences between humans and giants to notice Coal slip away.

Coal stood outside of Chalcedony's thick wooden door and straightened his brown pants and the white shirt he wore underneath his green jerkin. He ran a hand over his braids and noticed one of them had unraveled. Cursing under his breath, he quickly re-braided the stray kinky hair. Satisfied he was presentable, he knocked on the door.

"Who is it?" asked a gruff voice from inside the room. It was Chalcedony's royal advisor, Madoc. Coal was convinced that Madoc's primary goal in life involved making Coal miserable.

"It's me," Coal said in his most formal voice. "Legacy told me that Chalcedony is looking for me."

The door opened, and Princess Chalcedony stood on the other side. "Legacy's right. I am looking for you." She wore a black sleeveless shirt and matching pants that were only a few shades darker than her brown skin.

Coal bowed, bending low at the waist while happiness surged in his chest at the sight of his oldest friend.

"How can I help you, Princess?" he asked.

"Come in." She stepped back from the door, her muscular arms flexing as she motioned for him to step into the room. "Since when do you bow or call me princess?"

Since last week, when Madoc lectured me for ten minutes about properly addressing a future queen, Coal wanted to say, but instead, he kept quiet. The less he said, the less Madoc could use against him when Chalcedony left.

Once he stepped in the room, he saw there were three other fey sitting around the table in Chalcedony's office. Madoc sat closest to the door, scribbling on a sheet of paper. He scoffed at Coal before he turned back towards the table.

"If I am no longer needed, I'll be retiring to my room," said Binti, the female waif who had been sitting at the end of the table. She had a jumbled network of tiny blue veins that showed underneath her pale translucent skin. As she stood from the table, the loose pink dress she wore buckled around knobby knees before she pulled it down.

Binti and her twin brother acted as a tether between the two realms. If a rogue fey used magic in the human realm, her brother felt it. Through the link the siblings shared, her brother would let Binti know. Then, Binti would alert Chalcedony in the fey realm.

"Go ahead," Princess Chalcedony said. "Thanks for your help."

Binti nodded briefly at Chalcedony as she walked away from the table and towards the door. Coal shivered as she passed. The waif lowered the temperature of any room by five degrees just by her presence. They were rumored to be children of reapers sent into the physical world to live until they replaced their parents as harvesters of souls.

Motion next to Chalcedony caught his attention. His eyes were drawn to the blonde, blue-eyed elf standing next to Chalcedony.

Tetrick.

Chalcedony had spent the past two years with the high-born elf. He was appointed by his mother, Queen Tasla, to teach Chalcedony how to patrol her part of the human realm for fey who were there illegally. "Are you sure you wouldn't like me to escort you, Princess?" Tetrick asked.

As usual, the royal elf paid Coal no attention. Coal didn't know if it was better to be ignored and made to feel like he wasn't worth a second thought, or to be constantly ridiculed and belittled like Madoc treated him.

"No, thank you, Tetrick," Chalcedony answered.

"You should let him escort you," Madoc said with a tone that suggested it was more of an order than a choice.

"No," Chalcedony said with such intensity that her long, sharp incisors were visible. "But thank you anyway," she said to Tetrick, her temper back under control.

"Very well, Princess." Tetrick bowed, and then the elf disappeared as if he'd never been there.

"You should have let him take you," Madoc said.

"Take you where?" Coal asked. "I thought we had plans for today."

"We do." Chalcedony's red eyes were wide with joy. "It's a surprise. But first, go get your clothes. Then, I'll meet you upstairs in my room."

"What clothes?" Coal asked, confused. She'd changed from all business to playful so quickly it took Coal a moment to adjust.

"The ones you brought back from the human realm."

Coal hesitated. He was five the last time he'd worn those clothes. "Why?"

"You should not question a princess's orders," Madoc said.

Chalcedony huffed and turned to Madoc.

"You're dismissed, Madoc," Chalcedony ordered.

Madoc shot Coal a hateful look before he bowed towards Princess Chalcedony and left the room.

"Don't worry about him. He's in a bad mood."

"He's been in a bad mood for eleven years," Coal said. "I think it's safe to say he just really hates me."

"He doesn't hate you. He treats you just like he treats everybody else."

"Really?" Coal asked with a raised eyebrow.

"Okay, he may dislike you a little bit. Go, and meet me upstairs."

"But—" he began.

"No more questions or you'll spoil the surprise. Just go get them." Her voice was full of joy and mischief. He'd missed it. He'd missed her.

Coal bit his lip, stifling his next question before he left the room.

What could she possibly want with his human clothes? They were all he had that proved where he'd come from, but he hadn't touched or thought about them in years.

Coal stood at Chalcedony's bedroom door a few minutes later, holding a ragged shirt and a pair of pants.

The door stood open, but the room seemed empty until Chalcedony stepped from behind her dressing screen. He almost dropped his bundle when he saw her wearing a pair of blue pants and a yellow shirt. Human clothes.

"What are you wearing? How did you get those?" he asked.

"Jeans and a T-shirt, the items you have in your hands, are very common clothes in the human realm."

"But why are you wearing them?" he asked.

"It's a surprise. Give me yours, and I'll fix them for you."

She took his clothes, placed them on her bed and whispered over them. As she spoke, the holes in the shirt became smaller until they disappeared. The material stretched, becoming longer and wider. She worked the same magic with his pants.

"Wow, you could be a tailor. That'll come in handy if the giants decide to attack the dwarves."

"Ha ha." Chalcedony smiled in triumph. "Tetrick taught me this two days ago. I'm discovering more abilities the closer I get to my coronation."

He'd always been jealous of Chalcedony's ability to wield magic. Over the years, he'd gotten much better at hiding his envy, but still, every time he saw Tetrick and Chalcedony together, the jealousy and longing returned. Tetrick was strong, powerful, and able to phase in and out of most places anytime he wanted. He was everything Coal wasn't.

"Fine, you can lengthen clothes, but why do we need to wear them?" Coal asked.

"Stop asking questions and relax. I promise you won't be disappointed."

She waved her hand and an invisible force pushed him backward. She'd learned to move things years ago, but it wasn't until recently, that she could move anything heavier than a sheet of paper.

"Okay, okay. I won't ask any more questions. I can walk the rest of the way myself."

"Thank you." She lowered her hand, and the force disappeared from his chest. "Be careful back there. I don't want you ending up somewhere you shouldn't."

Reluctantly, but of his own free will, he walked behind the screen with his clothes.

A wave of nostalgia washed over Coal as he remembered the last time he'd ducked behind the screen. It served as Chalcedony's secret portal and her escape route if Legacy was ever invaded, which hadn't happened in over one hundred years. It was one of the best kept secrets in Everleaf. As children, they would travel through the screen pretending to hunt for treasure in the forest while everyone slept.

"So, what do you think?" Coal walked out from behind the screen. He didn't like the feel of the stiff fabric against his skin, but the clothes fit.

She stared, eyes narrowed.

"Did I put them on right?" he asked, feeling self-conscious under her intense gaze.

"You look fine." She smiled. "You look really good, actually."

"Um, thanks." If she liked them, he decided, they couldn't be all bad. "So are you going to tell me why we're dressed like this?"

"Nope." She wrapped a black cloak around her lean shoulders and then handed him an extra one lying on her bed. "Wrap up. I don't want anyone asking too many questions."

Coal followed her out of the room while he tried to hide his excitement and curiosity. His joy disappeared when he saw Madoc at the bottom of the stairs talking to Ambassador Eli. Madoc turned when he saw Chalcedony and Coal.

"You're not taking your shadows?" Madoc asked, cocking a bushy black and gray eyebrow.

"I know how to protect myself."

"Your pride will get you killed. Take your shadows. I'm sure they would appreciate the exercise."

She rolled her eyes. "No. You have to start trusting me."

"Traipsing through the human realm without your shadows is not something a queen would do."

"We're going to the human realm?" Coal blurted.

"Damn it, Madoc!" Chalcedony exclaimed. "I told you it was a surprise."

Madoc shrugged. "Take your shadows."

Chalcedony answered with a sneer before she stormed out of Legacy.

Coal followed behind Chalcedony while his mind raced. She chattered away, but he couldn't focus. Several moments passed before he asked, "Why didn't you tell me we were going to the human realm?"

"It was a surprise. Surprise!" She wore a mischievous grin that made her red eyes sparkle.

In any other situation, Chalcedony's good mood would have been contagious, but he'd been in the fey realm since he was five, and he'd never left Everleaf. He didn't know whether to be scared or excited.

"Why are we going? I've never asked to go there." Madoc not arguing with Chalcedony about taking Coal was troubling. If he knew anything about the elf, it was that he hated Coal. Most especially, Madoc hated Chalcedony to be seen with Coal outside of Legacy. His disapproval had grown more venomous over the past year.

"Are you going to leave me there?" he asked, recalling what the sentries had said.

Chalcedony stopped and faced Coal. "Why would you say that?"

"You didn't answer my question." His heart raced while he waited for a response.

"More and more of my work is there. It's so different. Human tech can be destructive, but it's amazing. Every time I go there I think of you, and I wish you could see it. That's why we're going."

"What about Madoc?"

"Don't worry about him. Do you really think I'd just leave you in the human realm without telling you?"

"No, I don't. It's just—"

"Coal, I've been tracking rogue fey in the human realm and dealing with serious situations for weeks," she said with desperation in her voice. "I want to have fun. I swear on my mother's sword that is the only reason why we're going."

He decided to believe her. But the twitching in the corner of her lips told Coal she was hiding something. "How are we going to the human realm without Tetrick? Don't you need him to phase us there?"

Chalcedony shrugged and continued walking. "No, we don't need Tetrick."

"Are we taking the dragons?" Coal asked, his curiosity piquing.

"No, we're not flying. We're taking the horses most of the way."

"You're not going to tell me, are you?" Coal asked as they entered the stable.

"Nope."

He smirked. "I didn't think so."

"Just relax," Chalcedony said. "You'll have fun. I promise."

"Are you really going to let them go to the human realm alone?" Ambassador Eli asked Madoc once Chalcedony and Coal had left.

"She may only be seventeen, but she's smart and one of the strongest in her line. I doubt anyone can hurt her except for a queen."

"Are you sure you're not overestimating her?" Ambassador Eli asked.

"I may be, but there is only so much I can do." Madoc faced the dwarf. Many dwarven ambassadors had passed through Legacy, and everyone had hated the bureaucratic process, except for Ambassador Eli. To Madoc's surprise, the dwarf seemed just as concerned for Everleaf as he was for protecting his people's fortunes and trade routes.

Ambassador Eli stroked his chin with a short, hairy finger. The dwarf had never worked in the mines so he was slim, instead of bulky and muscular. "I've been hesitant to bring this up, but you should know that most fey in Everleaf have begun to talk about the queenling and her human boy. There are rumors he is destined to become her lover and rule beside her."

"I am well aware of the rumors. That will never happen."

"What are your plans for him? I expected you to have gotten rid of him long before now."

"Chalcedony is supposed to leave the boy in the human realm while they're there."

Ambassador Eli exhaled. "That's a relief."

Madoc turned back towards the window. Chalcedony and the boy were on horseback, leaving through the gates. "But she lied to me. She is not going to leave him there. She is still too attached to him."

"Then, you need to get rid of him," Ambassador Eli said, his voice lifting.

Madoc watched them until they disappeared from sight. "I can't. The boy will play a significant role in Princess Chalcedony becoming a formidable queen."

"How can you be so sure?" Ambassador Eli asked, his tone full of doubt.

"I had a few truthsayers look into it. They all said the same thing. He's meant to stay until he decides to leave on his own."

The dwarf scowled. "Isn't it your job to make her a great queen?"

"Like I said, I can only do so much. I've shown her the best and the worst duties of being a queen, yet she remains a child. Her mother and grandmother …" Madoc hesitated, searching for the correct phrase, "had lost their innocence by her age. She is too happy, and it's all tied to the boy. Once he's gone, she'll lose her innocence. Besides, I can't kill him without her suspecting. She is young but intuitive. Out of resentment, she may hurt Everleaf. But if the thing she loves leaves on its own, then that is a different game altogether."

"The boy obviously worships her. He'll never leave without coercion."

"Ambassador Eli, I've been doing this for centuries. You have my word. The prophets have reassured me he won't be around much longer."

CHAPTER TWO

On horseback, Coal followed Chalcedony away from Legacy, through the town square and into the royal forest. After a few miles, they came upon a lake.

"We can leave the horses here. We have to walk the rest of the way." She bent down and put her hands in the water. "Remember this place?"

"Yeah." The sound of waves falling onto the shore mingled with the chirping of the birds and created a melody, making Coal feel like they were the only people left in the world. "We used to get in so much trouble for using your portal to come here to swim."

"Well, we're a little bit ahead of schedule. Do you want to go swimming?"

"We didn't bring any swim clothes."

She gave Coal a wicked grin. "Never stopped us before."

"That was a long time ago." Coal glanced nervously at Chalcedony's chest before he quickly averted his eyes. "We've changed since then."

Chalcedony tilted her head to the side. "We haven't changed that much."

She walked towards the lake and took off her clothes. At least she was wearing underwear. "You're trying to get me killed, aren't you? What if Madoc is watching?"

"Don't worry about Madoc. He promised he'd let me do anything I wanted today. And right now, this is what I want to do."

It had been a while since he'd been swimming, Coal thought, as he stripped down to his underclothes and followed her into the water.

After being picked up and thrown into the lake more times than she could count, Chalcedony ran out of the lake and sat on the grass. It had been a while since she'd done anything merely for fun, and she was glad Coal had warmed up to the idea of going to the human realm. The rift that had been growing between them over the past few months had finally closed.

Coal left the lake and sprinted towards her. She was seventeen, one year older than Coal, and until recently, she'd always towered over him. Her growth had slowed, and she would look this way for the next fifty years. But Coal continued to grow, and surprisingly, he'd caught up to her.

His ebony skin glistened in the midmorning sun as he stood above her. "You give up?" He laughed, one dimple forming on each cheek.

Madoc's Rule Number Eight: Never Admit Defeat. So, she changed the subject. "One of your braids has come undone." Chalcedony sat up and patted her lap. "Come here. I'll re-braid it."

He appeared as if he was going to refuse, but sat down and laid his damp head on her lap anyway. She undid the rest of the braid before passing her fingers through his thick hair to remove the kinks. She grabbed a small section and separated it into three before she began. "It took you forever and a day to learn how to braid. You were the worst student," Chalcedony said as she worked.

"I didn't want to learn. I liked it better when you did it."

"You have gotten better, though."

"I didn't have a choice. You've been too busy to do it," Coal said.

"Madoc thinks it's beneath me to braid my own hair. He most definitely didn't like it when I braided yours."

Coal tensed beneath her fingers at the mention of Madoc, so she changed the subject. "I love how your hair makes a halo around your head. For years, I tried to get my hair to match yours. But it's only darker, not curlier."

"Mmm," he murmured, sounding content and halfway asleep.

She couldn't blame him for being suspicious about this trip. He'd been correct. She was supposed to leave him in the human realm.

Agreeing to leave Coal behind was the only way she could get Madoc's approval to bring him along with her. Her coronation was in two weeks, and she needed to relax. Coal was the only person she relaxed with because he was the only person who didn't expect her to be perfect. Lying to her advisor wasn't something she did often, but there was only so much arguing she could do.

Coal's even breathing told her he'd dozed off. She'd forgotten how having his hair braided lulled him to sleep—once she'd learned how to avoid painful tangles.

She bent down and whispered in his ear. "I'm finished, Coal."

He turned his head, but he didn't open his eyes. She placed her hand on his forehead and studied his full lips, wondering if they were as soft as they seemed. She forced the thought out of her head and stood, causing Coal's head to drop from her lap and fall onto the ground.

"Ouch." He patted the side of his head. "What's wrong?"

"I'm sorry." Chalcedony staggered towards her clothes before she dressed. "We need to go. It's getting late."

Kissing Coal was the last thing she needed to be thinking about. She stared ahead, avoiding his gaze. *Everything's complicated enough.*

"What's wrong, Chaley?" Coal asked. Her relaxed, playful mood had vanished. What had happened while he slept? What had startled her?

"Nothing's wrong," she insisted. "We just need to hurry."

"Which way?" he asked, happy to be off the horse and traveling by foot. His butt and inner thighs were beginning to chafe from the saddle.

Chalcedony pointed to a bridge about a mile away through a small opening between the trees. "It's just over the bridge. I'll race you."

She sprinted away before he answered. Relieved she had cheered up, Coal didn't think to run after her until she had already left.

Halfway to the bridge, his legs burned and begged for him to stop. But instead of slowing, his pride pushed him faster and closer to Chalcedony. She twisted her head and grimaced when she saw him nearing. Chalcedony hated to lose. Elves were natural runners and predators, unlike humans, but he'd been running with Chalcedony and other elves for as long as he'd been here. He'd never won, but it never stopped him from trying.

He broke through the trees and into a clearing. The bridge was only a few feet away. With fewer obstacles, he was able to run fast enough to pass Chalcedony.

Looking to the side, he saw she was half a step behind him. He glanced back towards the bridge, just before colliding into it.

Chalcedony was on the bridge a fraction of a second later.

"I beat you," he gasped. "For the first time, I beat you."

"You nearly killed yourself trying to do it." She stood next to him, steady and calm. A thin layer of sweat prickled the skin above her top lip, but she wasn't breathing nearly as hard as him.

"I still beat you."

Chalcedony stepped behind Coal with a knife at his throat before he thought to move or defend himself.

"If we were fighting, you would have won a battle but lost the war. You no longer have any strength to combat me." The metal was cold and sharp against his neck.

Coal sobered, his breath finally under control. "Is that what you think?"

The knife pricked his skin. "Yes."

He grabbed Chalcedony's wrist and twisted, the knife fell to the ground. Then he pushed her onto the grass. "Hasn't Tetrick taught you not to underestimate your enemy?" he asked, standing above her, feeling cocky and triumphant.

Chalcedony swung her legs around, sweeping Coal's feet out from under him and sending him crashing onto his back beside her. She rolled onto him, laughing and straddling him with her knees. Her long, dark hair hung over the side of her face.

"Are we enemies?"

"Madoc says everyone is your enemy," Coal said.

"Is he right?" she asked. "Are you my enemy?"

Coal lifted himself onto his elbows and gazed into her eyes. "Chaley, I would die for you."

She bent down and touched her lips to his. He tasted salty, but the kiss was sweet, and it awakened a hunger that had been brewing for longer than she wanted to acknowledge.

CHAPTER THREE

One kiss couldn't hurt, right? Chalcedony thought, but then, she lost herself in the sensation.

Coal's hand brushed through her hair and sent tingles through her body.

"Princess!" someone shouted from behind. Chalcedony leaped off Coal. A royal guard stood a few feet away with his sword drawn.

"Are you okay, Princess?" the guard asked, looking from Chalcedony to Coal, and back again.

Bren, she remembered. One of Madoc's personal lackeys. He had ash-blonde hair with tawny-colored skin. His face was twisted in disgust and anger emanated from his pitch-black eyes.

Coal stepped slowly in front of Chalcedony. She wanted to tell him to stop. Bren was more likely to hurt him than her, but she didn't want to take her focus away from the guard. She felt for the hilt of the knife she hid underneath her shirt. "What are you doing here?" she asked, looking over Coal's shoulder.

"I was sent to patrol the forest." His hands shook, but he never lowered his sword.

"Are you going to attack me?" she asked with a haughty toss of her hair, hoping to draw his attention away from Coal. Bren flicked his gaze towards his weapon before he lowered it.

"I'm sorry, Princess. Of course, I would never hurt you."

Chalcedony relaxed, released the knife, and stepped out from behind Coal. "Since when do we patrol the forest?" she asked.

This forest hid the door to the human realm, but it was not guarded. Only a select few were supposed to know it existed. Patrolling it would only attract attention. Instead, an invisible barrier that prevented anyone from entering without permission protected the forest.

"Um," Bren stuttered, his eyes lowered.

"Madoc sent you, didn't he?"

"He … um, I was sent to patrol the door," Bren answered. She closed the space between the two of them.

"Look at me," she ordered. He met her gaze. "Are you lying to me?"

"No, Princess. I was assigned to patrol the forest today. I didn't know you would be here."

She studied him, searching for a lie. She was not a mind reader, but Tetrick had taught her to look past a fey's surface to recognize emotions and truth. Chalcedony saw fear, embarrassment, and disappointment, but there was no indication of a lie. Perhaps Madoc had set him up.

"Leave my forest before I have you banished for spying on me," Chalcedony ordered.

"Princess, I'm sorry. I swear I didn't know you would be here," Bren said, shaking.

"Leave now!"

"Yes, Princess."

He placed his sword in its sheath and stalked away. Once Bren disappeared between the trees, she walked towards the bridge.

"Are you alright?" Coal reached for her arm, but she flinched and moved away.

If she wanted Coal to live, she could never let him touch her again.

Coal followed her over the bridge. "Shouldn't we talk about what happened?"

"No. I shouldn't have done that."

He was about to argue with her, but everything was different, wrong. The air became denser, making it harder for Coal to breathe.

The trees, the grass, and even the sun were less vivid. It was as if he were looking through a smudged window.

"Chaley, where are we?"

Chalcedony met his gaze. "We're in the human realm."

"I didn't see any door."

She placed her hands on her hips. "If it could be seen, everyone would know where it was."

He turned in a slow circle, drinking in all he saw. The tree's brown bark was dull and washed out. The green leaves were watered down and muted. The grass cracked and moaned underneath his feet as if it were dying of thirst.

He had never stopped to listen to the everyday sounds of life; they'd always been in the background. But the singing and harmony of the forest had disappeared. This terrible silence made him feel as if something were missing.

The human realm, Coal decided, was a weak, lifeless version of the fey realm.

"Chalcedony, stop. I don't understand. How did we get here?"

She frowned, gazing into Coal's eyes as if deciding something. "Few fey or humans know this. You have to keep it secret."

"By now, you know you can trust me," Coal said.

She scanned the forest as if she were scared someone would overhear her. Satisfied they were alone, she said, "During the war, humans and fey decided to separate themselves so we couldn't destroy each other."

"I'm not stupid. I know that." His anxiousness over the new environment was giving away to agitation.

"They also created portals to connect the two realms, because, in spite of all the war and death, complete separation seemed unfathomable. Also, giants are humans. Every now and then, a giant will have a normal human child, and they wanted to be able to take those children to the human realm if they needed to."

"Ambassador Eli said giants weren't humans."

"Giants used to give birth to humans on a normal basis, but now that humans and giants don't interact as much, it's rare."

"Why haven't I heard of the portal before?"

"Because if everyone knew, the human realm would be overrun with rogue fey," Chalcedony said.

He decided to ask another question. "Why does the air smell so different?"

"Their technology pollutes the air." Chalcedony walked through the forest.

The ground was littered with broken tree branches that snapped underneath her feet. Coal marveled. He was in the human realm, his birthplace. Despite his curiosity and excitement, the image of the two of them kissing kept replaying in his mind. As he followed behind her, he wondered when it would happen again.

"Wait." She stopped so abruptly that he almost bumped into her.

She pulled a pouch from the pocket of her pants, placed her hand inside of it. Her fingers came out of the bag covered in a multi-hued powder. She recited a few words before she placed it in her mouth. Slowly, her long, sharp canine teeth widened and shortened. They lost their edge and became flat. Her slim pointed ears curved. Her large red eyes dimmed and turned black. She had changed into a human.

For a moment, Coal did not recognize the person standing in front of him. His vision adjusted as if it was adapting to the dark, and he saw past the illusion. She had swallowed glamour. Humans would look at Chalcedony and see the false image. For him, it was transparent, merely an overlay, barely hiding her true features.

"I'll be glad when I can change my teeth and ears. Tetrick says I should be able to do it soon. Then I won't have to use glamour every time I come here. Do I look human enough?" she asked.

"Yes," he answered. "But it's not as if I've seen many."

"Oh, right." Chalcedony rubbed the back of her neck. "Well, let's go look at some humans." She held out her hand. "We haven't gotten to the fun part yet."

He stared at her hand for a moment before he grabbed it and let her pull him out of the forest.

Cars. He remembered them from his childhood.

Red, yellow, blue, green, black. They sped by one after the other, leaving metallic fumes in their wake. Slowly he remembered other things, forgotten memories of concrete, laughing and running, and a woman's touch—soft and tender.

"Stay close." Chalcedony's voice pulled him out of his thoughts. "Are you okay?" she asked, staring at him intently.

He tried to put what he saw into words, but the memories were gone just as quickly as they'd appeared. "I'm fine." He looked around in an attempt to anchor himself. They were waiting for what he knew was a streetlight.

"Where are we going?" he asked.

"A coffee shop," Chalcedony said. "It's not far."

When the cars stopped, he followed her across the street. As they walked, Coal studied the people's faces. Most avoided eye contact, but some stared directly at him and smiled.

"We're here." She stopped at a building with a sign that read "Ground Beans." "It's a coffee shop. I figured this would be a nice place to sit and relax."

Coal shrugged, noting the hesitation in her voice. "This is your adventure. I'm just along for the ride."

She stood a little straighter, and he followed her into the shop. Coal sat in one of the wooden chairs next to a window while Chalcedony ordered. The noonday sun beamed onto the table and the smell of coffee and baked bread permeated the air. Chalcedony brought him coffee and a cream-filled pastry. For the second time that day, he was reminded how he hadn't had breakfast. He ate the pastry in three quick bites. He'd expected for it to be bland, like the dull colors of the human realm, but it tasted sweet and flavorful.

"I never get to do anything like this." Chalcedony bit into her pastry, chewed, and then swallowed. "I hunt rogue fey and then, we immediately go back home." She leaned back and smiled as the sunlight danced on her face.

"Why did you bring me here?" he asked.

Chalcedony stared out of the window at the crowded street. "I wanted to show you this. Most of the people here are college students. Look at how easy they live and how happy they are. They're a few years older than us, but they have no responsibilities. Their only job is to go to school. That's it."

Coal noticed half of the people in the shop had devices in front of their faces and wires connected to their ears. They didn't look happy. They spoke in high, grating voices, a sharp contrast to the husky and almost guttural sounds he had grown used to in the fey realm.

"I dream about running away and living here—maybe just the two of us," Chalcedony added.

"Why can't we?" Coal asked. He loved living around magic and being in the fey realm, but if living here meant that he would be able to be with Chalcedony, he would do it a thousand times over. He reached out to touch her hand, but she pulled away.

"Too many of my fey would die while Tetrick's mother and Queen Isis fought over Everleaf."

"Why can't you just leave everything to Madoc?" Coal asked, trying to hide his embarrassment at her rejection.

"No male shall rule. You know that. The other queens have only left me alone because it's against the law to rage war against a queenling. Besides, my mother made it clear before she died that my duty would always be to rule and protect Everleaf. I've never had an option, and neither will my oldest daughter. I'm cursed to reign, just as Madoc is cursed to serve."

"Hi," squeaked a small child wearing a pink dress and a tiara. Surprised, Coal and Chalcedony stared at the child, speechless.

"Hi," Chalcedony said, the first to recover.

"Are you a fairy princess?" the girl asked.

Chalcedony laughed nervously. "Why?"

"Because you have pointy ears. I'm a princess, too." The girl tapped her tiara and swung her waist-length jet-black hair from side to side. "I'm not a fairy, though. Are you?"

Chalcedony glanced briefly at Coal. "What's your name?"

"Elizabeth. I'm six." The girl smiled, showing a large gap where her two front teeth should've been. "Where did you come from?"

"I am from the land of the fey," Chalcedony said with a low mischievous tone.

"Fey like a fairy?" Elizabeth's eyes were wide with joy. "Can I go there with you?"

"Elizabeth!" Someone shouted from across the shop. A woman, an exact copy of Elizabeth, only taller and plumper, walked towards them. Behind her sat a baby strapped in a high chair banging a piece of bread against a plate.

"Momma, look. She's a fairy. See. She has pointy ears," Elizabeth said when the woman reached their table.

"She does not have pointy ears," her mother said with a strained smile before she faced Chalcedony. "I'm so sorry. She says some of the most incredible things sometimes."

Chalcedony said, "That's alright. She's not bothering us."

"Let's go, Lizzy." The woman pulled Elizabeth towards the table where the baby sat.

Chalcedony spun towards Coal. Her eyes glowed with elation. "I've been to the human realm dozens of times. Besides you, I've never met another human who saw through glamour. Never!"

Madoc sat in his office, hunched over his desk, trying to find the source of the pollution in the giants' water supply. He'd gone out himself to track the cause, but had found nothing. If it had only been poisoned once, the giants probably would have ignored it, but it had happened three times. They blamed the dwarves who lived and mined in the mountains upstream. Thankfully, neither the giants nor Madoc proved the dwarves had anything to do with it. The last thing they needed was a war.

A slow, hesitant tap at the door brought Madoc out of his thoughts. "What is it?" he asked, welcoming the distraction.

Bren stepped into Madoc's office. "Sir, I'm checking in from the forest."

Madoc leaned forward in his chair. "I'm listening,"

"They were there," Bren began. "I was hiding as you recommended, but when I saw them in a … questionable position, I had to interrupt and make sure the princess was not being harmed."

"What do you mean questionable position?"

Bren cleared his throat. "They were … they appeared to be kissing."

"It's either they were or they weren't." Madoc suppressed a smile, amused by Bren's obvious discomfort. Bren paused and lifted his head.

"They were kissing, sir."

A grin crept across Madoc's face. Well, they finally crossed the line. "What did the princess say when you interrupted them?"

"She was surprised and asked where I had come from."

"Did you tell her I sent you?"

"I told her you had ordered me to patrol the forest."

"And she believed you?" Madoc asked.

"Yes."

"Good." Few of his guards were so good at lying. "Did you tell anyone else about this?"

"No, sir," Bren said, recoiling as if he'd been insulted. "Of course not."

"Well." Madoc sat back in his chair. "Don't feel like you have to keep it a secret."

Bren grimaced and narrowed his eyes in confusion. Madoc crossed his arms across his chest.

"I want you to spread this rumor of them kissing. It may be a helpful catalyst to get the human out of this realm."

Bren nodded. "Yes, sir. I understand."

"Good. You're dismissed."

After Bren left, Madoc closed his eyes. He tried to predict where this relationship with Chalcedony and Coal would lead. It could only end one way: nowhere. He wanted to kill the boy to ensure that, but he trusted his prophets. They rarely foresaw anything, so when they did, he listened and obeyed. He felt change in the air. He had no idea what was coming, but he was looking forward to watching it play out.

Chalcedony couldn't stop staring at Elizabeth. The girl reminded her so much of Coal at that age.

"Chalcedony," Coal said.

She turned towards him. For a moment, she'd forgotten he'd come with her.

"You okay?" he asked.

"I'm fine." Coal was trying to look comfortable. But she'd known him for too long to be fooled. His shoulders were squared as if he was waiting for someone to start a fight with him. He gripped his mug as if it was the only thing between him and death.

"You don't like it here, do you?" Chalcedony asked.

"No," he answered without hesitation.

"Why?"

"I'm not sure. I was homeless before you found me. Maybe that has something to do with it. When we first arrived, I remembered a woman. I think she was my mother, but then she left me." Coal changed the subject. "What are we going to do about the kiss?"

She rubbed the back of her neck. She could dodge the question again, but he would just keep bringing it up. Besides, he was right. It needed to be addressed. "There is nothing we can do about it. Madoc will kill you if ..." she trailed off. "We have to forget it happened." She glanced at the ground, willing the memory of their kiss away. "We're best friends. That's all we can ever be."

"Queen Isis, in the south, has a human mate and no children." He stared at his cup.

"She's a hundred years older than me. No one doubts she's strong enough to fight for her lands. I don't have that luxury."

"Why don't you fight for what you want?" Coal pressed.

She couldn't let herself even think about being with him. The thought felt like a betrayal to her mother and all she'd worked for since birth. "Why did we have to grow up? It was so much simpler when we ran around Legacy all day without—"

"Without wanting to kiss each other in the middle of it," he said with a crooked smile.

"No." She laughed despite herself. "When we were younger, we spent all day together without everyone gossiping."

He sobered suddenly. "Are you going to leave me here?"

"I told you already. I would never do that. Do you want to stay?"

"No, I hate it here," he responded as if she'd accused him of stealing.

"Don't worry about it." Yes, it would solve everything, but the thought of being without him scared her. Out of the corner of her eye, Chalcedony saw Elizabeth waving goodbye as her mother hustled her out the door.

"Are you finished?" Chalcedony asked, standing. Coal placed his cup on the table and stood.

"Yes."

"Let's go." Chalcedony hurried out of the shop. Just as they bounded onto the street, Elizabeth and her family turned the corner. Chalcedony walked faster.

"Are we leaving now?" Coal matched Chalcedony's pace.

"Not yet."

"Then, where are we going?"

"You'll see," she answered, but she didn't really know herself. She wanted to talk to the girl again.

As Chalcedony expected, Elizabeth and her family didn't live far from the coffee shop. Humans drove most places, but not if they lived on a college campus. Elizabeth's mother unlocked the door to their apartment and stepped in. Chalcedony waited a few moments, and knocked.

"Why are we here?" Coal asked, with an impatient, accusatory tone.

"Shh."

"No. Why are we here?"

She knocked again, ignoring his burning gaze.

"Oh, hi? Did I forget something at the restaurant?" Elizabeth's mother asked after she opened the door.

"Yes," Chalcedony said. "Can we come in?"

"Um." She eyed Chalcedony and Coal. "What do you want?"

Before she lost her nerve, Chalcedony brought the pouch of glamour from under her shirt and blew the powder into the woman's face.

CHAPTER FOUR

When the glamour hit Elizabeth's mother, she flinched and blinked, trying to clear her eyes. After a long moment, she shook her head and refocused Chalcedony. The suspicious look she'd had earlier disappeared, replaced with a too-wide smile.

"What was that?" Coal asked.

"I'm glamouring her. That way, she'll have to do what I say," she said in a low, impatient voice.

"I'm sorry, I'm forgetting my manners. Come on in. My name is Deedee."

"Why are we here, Chaley?" he repeated, hesitant to step into the woman's home. Chalcedony ignored his question, grabbed his elbow and pulled him into the apartment.

The baby sat in the middle of the floor surrounded by toys. "Please excuse the mess. Between Elizabeth, her little brother, and my husband, who is a doctoral student at the university, I can't keep up with the housework." Deedee walked to the baby and picked him up. "What can I do for you guys?"

"Excuse us." Coal pulled Chalcedony to the side of the room, facing away from Deedee and the baby. "Why did you glamour her? Whatever you're doing, drop it and let's go home."

"She asked to come with us," Chalcedony said.

"Who? The girl?"

As if she read their mind, Elizabeth shrieked from behind them. "Fairy princess!"

Chalcedony faced away from Coal.

"Hi, Elizabeth."

"What are you doing here?" the girl asked with unrestrained joy.

"You said you wanted to come home with me, so I thought I'd ask your mom if it was okay." Chalcedony's voice was thick and sugary.

The girl gasped, sounding as if she was choking on air. "Really? I can come to fairyland with you?"

"Yep." Chalcedony nodded. "If your mom agrees."

"Momma, can I go?" Elizabeth begged, pulling on her mother's shirt.

"That doesn't sound like a good idea, Lizzy." Deedee's hands shook as she held the baby.

"But Momma, please!" Elizabeth begged.

"No, Lizzy," Deedee said, with a thin smile. The color had left her cheeks. Wrinkles appeared around her eyes. It seemed to Coal as if she'd had aged ten years in the few minutes they'd been there. "Besides, you don't want to put up with her. She's hyperactive. You'll be ready to bring her back after an hour."

"We don't mind." Chalcedony touched Deedee's shoulder. "You look tired. With Elizabeth gone, you'll be able to get some rest."

Deedee glanced around nervously as if she was thinking about running away, but whatever had been making her hesitate broke as she focused on Chalcedony again. "The two of them are such a handful. Elizabeth is so hyper, and I don't always have the time to give her the attention she needs."

"Please, can I go?" Elizabeth pleaded. "Please?"

"Yes, you can go." Deedee's eyes were empty as she stared straight ahead, hugging the wriggling baby tighter.

Coal searched her face for some sign of resistance, but the glamour had completely pacified her.

"Oooh, thank you! Thank you, Momma! I'll be good. I promise. I have to get my princess stuff. I'll be right back," Elizabeth said, running into the back of their house.

"Chaley," Coal said, feeling as if he was a monster in someone's nightmare. "What are you doing?"

"She wants to come." Chalcedony turned her back to him just as Elizabeth re-emerged from her room. "Are you ready?" Chalcedony asked.

Elizabeth curtsied. "Yes, Princess." She gave her mother a hug. "Don't worry, Momma. I'll be extra good. I promise."

"She'll be completely safe," Chalcedony said.

"Bye, sweetie. I love you," Deedee replied. Her eyes never focused on Elizabeth. They were somewhere else, lifeless.

Elizabeth and Chalcedony walked out the door and down the stairs. They never glanced back, but Coal did.

He watched as Deedee held the restless baby. She glanced past Coal as if he didn't exist. The baby in her arms cried, and she cooed at him mechanically before she closed the door.

He ran after Chalcedony. They hadn't made it far in the jumble of concrete buildings.

"Chaley, what are you doing? It's against the human–fey treaty to take a human without permission."

"I didn't take her against her will. She wanted to come."

"But her mom—"

"The treaty says humans can't be taken against their will or without royal permission," Chalcedony said. "You wanted to come. Didn't you Elizabeth?"

"Yes." The child nodded.

Coal grabbed Chalcedony's hand, forcing her to stop. "She's just a little girl. She doesn't know what she wants," he said under his breath so Elizabeth couldn't hear.

"Let go of me, Coal," Chalcedony snapped, with barely disguised anger.

"No. You need to listen. Madoc will kill both of us if you bring another human to the fey realm."

"Let go of my arm," Chalcedony commanded. "I know what I'm doing."

They locked gazes, silently fighting each other.

"We have to go. We've been gone too long." Chalcedony held Elizabeth's hand and sprinted away. Elizabeth ran with her, giggling as if she and Chalcedony were best friends.

The trek took twice as long with Elizabeth with them. By the time they'd found their horses and reached the forest, Elizabeth was sleeping peacefully against Chalcedony's chest, as night had completely engulfed Everleaf.

"Thank goodness she's finally asleep. She talks too much," Coal said.

"She's just excited," Chalcedony replied, with a hint of exhaustion in her voice. "You were the same way when you first arrived."

"I'm nothing like her."

When they approached the night market, his stomach flipped. They'd always been prohibited from visiting the square after dusk. It was one of the few rules Madoc had imposed that both he and Chalcedony had followed. It was friendly during the day, but at night, the predators ventured out in search of prey.

"I'm going to conceal myself. I don't want anyone to see me with Elizabeth." She brought the collar of the cloak to her mouth and spoke into it. A second later, she disappeared, along with Elizabeth and her horse.

He didn't have to ask why she wanted to be invisible. Humans in Everleaf were forbidden without royal permission. And thanks to Madoc, they never gave permission. Chalcedony was abusing her power, and she didn't want anyone to know it.

"Shouldn't we go around the market?" Coal looked towards the spot where Chalcedony had just been.

"No," she said. "I'm tired. That would take too long."

Coal bit his lip. "But—"

"You'll be fine. I'll make myself visible again if you run into any trouble."

Looking around, Coal's throat tightened with uneasiness while he remembered all of the horror stories told about this place. A moment later, hoof prints appeared in the grass, and he followed them into the market.

Music and voices from all directions mingled in an uneasy cadence. During the day, vendors sold milk, eggs, cheese, and other harmless goods. Some even sold weak potions that contained more herbs than magic.

Halfway through, he passed a group of fey completely covered in black clothing except for their eyes. They stood motionless behind an elven vendor.

"Do you need a hired sword?" the vendor asked.

"No," Coal answered.

"I also have thieves," the elf said. "Is there something you have been coveting, human? I could get it for you."

Coal shook his head and continued, wondering how many would accept the professional thief's offer. Further on, he saw an auburn-haired dwarf explaining to an elf how the poison-laced edges of her weapons worked.

He covered his nose with his shirt when he passed the pungent dead bodies of elves, dwarves, and the torso of a giant at the butcher's booth. It was illegal to kill fey for meat, but if someone died, their family could choose to sell it to the weavers for experimentation or, as in this case, sell the cadaver to a butcher.

"I smell humans," Coal heard someone say just as he'd passed the butcher's booth.

A seven-foot-tall troll with green skin sniffed the air. The troll looked past where Coal knew Chalcedony and Elizabeth were, paused for a moment, and settled his gaze onto Coal.

"Yes," it said, "I do smell human." He took one long stride and blocked Coal's path. He was shirtless, but he wore a pair of black pants that stopped before his ankles.

"Let me pass." Coal tried to control his fear and his nervous horse. The troll answered with a wide, toothy grin. For an instant, Coal saw himself strung up, lifeless and gutted, at the butcher's booth.

The troll stepped closer and sniffed the air once again. "You smell good."

The troll's breath reeked of rot despite his perfect white teeth.

"You don't," Coal said.

The troll snarled, distorting its features into something even more grotesque. Coal glanced ahead, clenching the horse's reins with sweaty hands.

"That's royal property. Leave it be," said a familiar voice, startling both Coal and the troll.

Coal recognized the black beast from a royal party two years ago. It had been the only pooka Coal had ever seen. Pookas resembled horses, except they had red glowing eyes and large ears that stuck straight out to the side. Sharp horns extended above his ears and arched backward.

"This is the queenling's legendary human toy?" the troll asked.

"Yeah, so leave it alone. The last thing we need is Madoc and the princess breathing down our necks."

The troll frowned. "Damn. I was hungry." He wiped spittle from his chin as he moved from Coal's path.

"There are dealers here who specialize in human meat." The pooka said to the troll before he turned to Coal. "You shouldn't be out at night, boy."

Coal nodded. His heart was beating too fast to do anything more. He nudged his horse forward and made a mental note to start carrying a sword. He was "royal property," or so they called him, but he needed to take care of himself. What if the pooka hadn't been there? Chalcedony would have interrupted, but she had probably already cleared the market. He'd have been dead by the time she decided to look for him.

From the corner of his eyes, he saw a group of pixies dancing in circles. All thought of danger disappeared as he watched. The pixies were slightly taller than most dwarves. When they flew, beautiful brightly colored lights trailed behind them, glowing in the night. They flew in circles, stopping periodically to sway their hips as patrons dropped coins into their coffers. Their bare chests were covered in glitter that shimmered while they danced to a flute played by a satyr.

He dug into his pocket for a gold piece to throw into their cup.

"Well, Coal. I never took you for one to be so easily fooled by pixie magic."

Pulled back to reality by a familiar voice, Coal glanced down and saw Sara, a moon elf. Her hair glowed silver in the moonlight as she patted his horse.

"Hi, Sara." He laughed, embarrassed. "I didn't know pixies were so beautiful." Coal finally understood why people allowed themselves to be enchanted by them. The pleasure of watching them dance outweighed the loss of a few gold coins. He started to glance back at the pixies, but Sara cleared her throat.

"They are not beautiful, they're enchanting. There is a difference," Sara said. Her hair was pulled back, revealing the sharp tip of her ears.

"You're right." Coal tried to clear his mind of the pixies by changing the subject. "You working tonight?"

Sara was one of the few fey who hadn't teased him for being a human. Once, he tried to bring Sara and Chalcedony together, but Chalcedony instantly disliked her. If Coal was being honest with himself, he hadn't been surprised; Chalcedony didn't get along with anyone when they were younger, besides Madoc.

"Yes. There's a full moon. It's a perfect night to scope out losers and vagrants. You know, I'll dance for you if you really want to give your money away. No cheap magic involved."

Coal lifted his eyebrows and gaped. Sara's parents owned a booth that contracted out private dancers, but as far as he knew, Sara wasn't one of them.

"Coal, you are easily distracted." Chalcedony appeared out of nowhere with Elizabeth still hidden underneath her cloak. He thought she'd left him and was on his way to Legacy.

"I'm sorry, Princess," Sara said, head bowed. "I didn't know you were there."

Chalcedony took her gaze from Sara and glared at Coal. "Let's go," she demanded before she rode away. The crowd had grown the instant she'd appeared, and it parted just as quickly as she passed.

"She's just as friendly as she was when we were kids," Sara said, her voice laced with sarcasm.

"I'm sorry. We're in a rush," Coal said, embarrassed by the way Chalcedony had ignored Sara.

"Don't worry about it. You'd better go before you get in trouble." She patted his horse before gently pushing it away.

"I'll see you later," Coal said, but Sara had already disappeared into the crowd.

"Was that Sara?" Chalcedony asked once they'd left the market.

"Yes."

"Is that your girlfriend?" she asked.

"You know Sara and I are only friends."

"Why did she offer to dance for you?"

"She was joking." *I think.*

"I don't think she was."

"How would I have a girlfriend without you knowing?" Coal asked.

"I haven't been home much. There are probably lots of things you aren't telling me."

CHAPTER FIVE

Chalcedony stood before Legacy's entrance with Elizabeth's arms wrapped around her neck and the girl's legs clinging awkwardly around her waist.

One of the two sentries at the door gasped when she saw Chalcedony carrying Elizabeth. However, both were immobile. Chalcedony cleared her throat, and the sentries quickly opened the door. They were just for show. Legacy wouldn't allow anyone to enter if they didn't have permission to be there, but soldiers who lost control as easily as these needed more training. Chalcedony made a mental note to have Djamel replace them.

She stared at the open door. She felt like a child sneaking into the house, hoping her mother wasn't awake.

"Are we going in?" Coal asked, eyebrows arched.

Mouth dry, Chalcedony nodded and shifted Elizabeth to her other shoulder. The girl moaned but stayed asleep.

They were almost to the stairs that led to her room. For a few blissful moments, Chalcedony thought she'd get through the night without having to deal with Madoc.

"Child, you almost missed the door." A familiar voice in the darkness stopped Coal dead in his tracks.

"We made it in plenty of time," Chalcedony said.

Madoc sat in a chair in the far corner of the dark room with a book in his lap. His eyes were incredible, even for an elf. He could read in complete darkness, where most elves only made out shapes.

"What do you have in your arms?" Madoc asked. He snapped his fingers and the fire lamps came on.

No point in lying. Chalcedony shifted so Madoc saw Elizabeth.

Suddenly, he was standing right in front of her. She had never seen him move so fast. But that was Madoc. He never let you know what his true strengths were.

"This is the reason you were so anxious to go to the human realm? You wanted to steal a human child?" he asked. The words came so quick she barely understood him.

"I didn't steal her. She wanted to come."

Madoc pointed a finger in her face. "That does not mean you take it home with you. Humans are not allowed here unless royal permission has been granted."

Chalcedony took a deep breath. "I give the royal permission." She walked up the stairs to her room.

"You are not above the law, Chalcedony!" Madoc screamed.

Chalcedony stopped, waiting to see if Madoc had awakened Elizabeth. He hadn't. She snored as if she were in her own bed instead of being held awkwardly in Chalcedony's arms.

"I did not break any laws." She couldn't remember the last time she'd seen Madoc so angry. He'd always told her that anger was a sign of weakness.

"Chalcedony!"

"Madoc, I'm tired," Chalcedony whispered. "We can argue about this tomorrow."

"This won't take long."

Chalcedony grimaced. His tone had changed. He sounded more worried than angry. *Damn.* It was much easier to walk away from anger than concern. "Coal, will you take Lizzy to your room until I come for her?"

"Of course, Princess," Coal said, as though he were a servant. She hated when Coal changed in front of Madoc. He seemed to fold into himself and become a shadow of the person he truly was.

Once Coal and Elizabeth were gone, she moved to the chair next to where Madoc had been sitting. He followed and sat beside her. She forced herself not to buckle underneath the steely gaze.

"Chalcedony, you're about to be queen. Instead of becoming more responsible, you are becoming reckless. If you want to delay your coronation for a year or so, we can probably—"

She cut him off. "We can't delay my coronation. The other queens are waiting for me to slip. A delay would be the sign that they're looking for." Chalcedony paused, willing her breathing to slow. "I'm fine."

She wasn't fine. She was scared. Scared to lead. Scared she would never be as good as her mother. Scared to lose her best friend. But she couldn't tell him. Madoc, despite his concern for her, only cared for Everleaf. He didn't understand fear. He didn't understand loneliness. He only existed to serve.

Chalcedony stood. "I'm fine, Madoc," she repeated. "I know it was irresponsible to bring another human here, but you said Coal has to leave. He is my only friend. I can't give him up without having something else to take his place." Chalcedony waited to see if Madoc would disagree. When he remained silent, she continued. "I've learned a lot over the past few years. I've excelled at every task you've given me. I'm ready to be queen. I'm ready to lead. You don't have to worry about me."

She wasn't ready to lead, but she wasn't strong enough to admit it out loud.

Madoc stood, book in hand. "Ready or not, you will be queen. The mystery is whether you will be the last of your line to rule."

She fought to hold his gaze while she kept her voice from trembling. "I will be a great queen."

"Not if you surround yourself with humans. They are weak and will make you weak," Madoc said before he walked away.

She opened her mouth to refute his words, but he was gone before she thought of something to say. He didn't know what he was talking about. She needed something other than duty. Coal had been the only person in her life who didn't make her feel like she was supposed to be something more than what she was. The girl would make losing Coal easier.

Coal awoke with the awareness that he'd overslept and was late for another session with Grigory. He rolled over to find Elizabeth and Chalcedony sleeping in his bed. The memories of traveling to the human realm and bringing back Lizzy flooded back.

He stared over Elizabeth's head at Chalcedony and thought of the kiss that could never happen again. When they were younger, they'd often slept together, playing until they reluctantly fell asleep, but now they were older. He ran his fingers through Chalcedony's hair and she slowly opened her eyes. "You should probably leave before Madoc starts looking for you."

A smile crept across her face. "And he kills you for having me in your bed."

He laughed. "Yeah, that too."

Chalcedony stood, still wearing her human clothes, and yawned. She picked up the sleeping child, and they left.

It seems, Coal thought, as he sat with his legs crossed on his bed, staring at the closed door as if the kiss never happened at all.

"What do you think they'll do with Coal?" The cook's deep voice echoed through the kitchen door.

"I heard he was supposed to stay in the human realm, but he refused to leave the princess. You see how he pouts whenever she's gone. He is too beguiled to let her go," Fatou, the maid said.

Her voice was lower. Coal had to strain to hear it.

"A guard caught them kissing yesterday."

"That's impossible. Madoc would have him drawn and quartered if that was the case."

"It's happened before," Fatou insisted. "Look at Queen Isis and her human."

"Why would she bring another human here if it's not to replace the old one?"

"Lovers or not, Madoc is not going to let that boy stay," Masson said.

Coal had hoped to get something to eat before he went to help Grigory with Chalcedony's sword, but instead, he'd accidentally come upon the kitchen staff gossiping. No longer hungry, he turned away and walked straight into Madoc.

"Excuse me, sir." Coal stepped back towards the kitchen. Facing gossiping servants was much better than dealing with Madoc.

"Coal, can I speak to you?"

"I'm late for a meeting with Grigory."

"That can wait." Taken off guard, Coal let the elf pull him away.

They sat across from each other in Madoc's private office. When Coal couldn't stand the silence any longer, he spoke. "I'm late for—"

"Why didn't you stay in the human realm?" Madoc interrupted.

Coal swallowed, trying to moisten his dry mouth. "Chaley didn't want me to."

"You should have stayed." Madoc leaned forward. "You do not belong here." He stressed each word as if speaking slowly would suddenly make Coal agree with him.

Coal lowered his head and rubbed his eyes, suddenly exhausted. "This is my home," Coal began. "I belong here just as much as you."

"I have lived here for centuries. I have worked for this family all of my life. Don't ever compare yourself to me. You are here on the whim of a young girl."

Coal remained motionless, refusing to believe Madoc's words.

Madoc sat back and continued. "The princess will be an especially young queen. The other queens have agreed to leave her alone until her coronation, but I believe they are planning to take her lands as soon as she is officially crowned. They will be looking for weaknesses to exploit, and they will try to turn her fey against her. Despite Chalcedony's awkwardness, she is loved by her fey. Before, everyone considered her affection for you as a lovable quirk. But now, people are wondering if she plans to rule with you as her mate."

"Chaley and I are just friends. That's all we have ever been."

"Don't sit there and lie to me. I know about your tryst on the way to the human realm."

He knew. Fear kicked him in the gut, but Coal forced himself to remain calm. "I know Chaley and I will never be together."

"What are you going to do? Wait on her for the rest of your life? You cannot be by her side. She brought that child here as your replacement. Once you saw that, why did you come back?"

Was that true?

"Grigory has offered me a full apprenticeship," Coal answered. "I plan on accepting the offer." He hadn't thought to accept the offer until now.

"I repeat," Madoc said through clenched teeth, "you don't belong here. Not as Chalcedony's friend nor as an apprentice to the mixed breed."

Am I really that much of a threat?

"I'm here because Chaley wants me here. I would have stayed in the human realm if she had asked me to."

"You don't belong here!" Madoc slammed his fist onto the desk.

Coal jumped, shocked by the sudden burst of anger.

The elf took a deep breath. "After her coronation, she will need an heir as soon as possible. She will have to choose a mate. Have you thought about how it would feel to see her with someone else? The biggest favor you can do for yourself is leave. An apprenticeship will not take you far enough away."

"Chaley and I are only friends. The kiss was a mistake. It was nothing." The words were poison on his tongue.

"Your presence is the danger!" Madoc's amber eyes were filled with anger and his long, yellowed incisors were bared. He looked as if he was about to tear Coal apart.

Coal sat back, trying to put as much distance between himself and Madoc as possible. Every instinct told him to leave, run away, but Coal refused. Madoc would have to kill him first.

Why hadn't Madoc killed him? He knew about the kiss. If Madoc could touch him, he would have done it by now. All Madoc could do was deliver empty threats.

Coal stood with his chest out, towering over the seated elf. "I belong here. If Chaley wants me to leave, I'll leave. Until then, the fey realm is my home." He stalked out of the room, with the sound of his heartbeat drowning out any protests Madoc could have had.

A sword flew past his shoulder and into the wall the moment he strode into Grigory's shop.

"You're late," Grigory said, holding his own sword, poised and ready to fight.

"Sorry, I woke up late." On any other day, a sword coming within an inch of his face would have scared him, but after facing Madoc, it didn't register. Coal grabbed the hilt of the sword and pulled it out of the wall before he faced Grigory. Grigory aimed his sword at Coal's chest, but Coal jumped back, expecting the attack. He stared intently at Grigory while he swung his blade with brutal force.

Grigory was gone long before the blade ever reached its destination.

Already Coal felt better, elated almost, as he fought and allowed the sword to channel his anger.

After a few parries and thrusts, they stood face to face once again.

"I hear we have a new human at Legacy," Grigory said. He hadn't shaved in two days and his beard already looked thick.

"For someone who hardly gets visitors, you sure know all of the gossip."

"Soldiers gossip more than the town wives."

The sword pulsated in Coal's hands, wanting to attack. He tuned it out and waited for Grigory's next move.

"I also heard that you were sent back to the human realm. I didn't expect you to be here today."

Growing impatient, Coal stepped forward and aimed the sword at Grigory's side. "Everleaf is my home. I'm not going anywhere."

Grigory dodged. He met Coal's attack with a speed Coal barely registered. "Many fey disagree with you."

"The only opinion that matters is Chaley's, and she wants me here." Coal swept around and came at Grigory's other side.

Grigory did not meet his attack this time, he simply moved out of Coal's way and stepped his foot out. Too late to react, Coal tripped.

As Coal tried to stand, Grigory put his foot on Coal's back, pushing him back to the ground. "Anger is good, especially if it's righteous, but you must control it just as you must control a weapon. Unleashed anger will get you killed just as if you've fallen onto your own sword."

Coal nodded, letting his anger dissipate.

Grigory removed his foot. "How is the sword handling?" he asked.

Coal stretched, still feeling the imprint where Grigory's foot had been. "Fine."

"It doesn't seem right to me." Grigory inspected the sword. "Something is off."

"It's fine with me. It's smooth. No vibrations." Coal laughed. "It actually seemed happy to see me today."

Grigory frowned. "What do you mean it felt happy?"

"I'm not sure. I think it was waiting for me."

"You should not be able to register its feelings. For one, you're human. Two, you're not its wielder, and three, you haven't been bonded to it."

"Well … uhh … I've been feeling it since yesterday."

"Why didn't you say anything?"

"I thought that was a good thing," Coal answered.

"Let's trade swords. We'll see if I have that same sensation."

"But first," Coal said, "is the offer for a full apprenticeship still open?"

Grigory paused. "Are you accepting it?"

"I want to accept." Coal licked his lips. "But I need to know you're not offering me the apprenticeship out of pity. I'm human. I can't do magic, so I'll never be as great as you."

Madoc was right about one thing at least. He needed to be away from Chalcedony. If his presence endangered her, he would leave. In the meanwhile, apprenticing with Grigory would move Coal out of Legacy and away from Chalcedony. That should be enough to pacify Madoc and the gossips.

Grigory rested his hands on the hilt of his sword. "You're a coddled, lovesick human. You do not deserve my pity."

Coal ignored the sting in Grigory's last words and bent to one knee. "It would be an honor to be your apprentice, Master."

CHAPTER SIX

Chalcedony basked in the sunlight in the room adjacent to her bedroom. She was half-listening to Djamel's updates on the last batch of rogue fey they'd caught in the human realm.

In truth, she was waiting for Elizabeth to wake up. Bringing the child to Everleaf had felt right. Just as it had when she'd found Coal. Movement out of the corner of her eye caught Chalcedony's attention. Elizabeth entered with her hair disheveled on one side, rubbing her eyes and yawning.

"Good Afternoon, Lizzy. Welcome to Everleaf," Chalcedony said eagerly.

"I made it?" Elizabeth asked, her weariness disappearing. "I'm really in fairyland?"

"Yes." Chalcedony inwardly cringed at the term fairyland.

Elizabeth ran to Chalcedony and leaped into her arms. "Thank you for bringing me here. Thank you. Thank you." She kissed Chalcedony's cheek repeatedly, before she paused, finally realizing Djamel was in the room. "Is this your prince?"

"No. This is Djamel. He is one of my shadow guards." Chalcedony remembered the human term for a shadow was different.

"Hello, Elizabeth," Djamel said. His voice was like ice cream, sweet and thick.

Elizabeth studied Djamel, staring him up and down. "He is much too princely to be a guard. Are you secretly in love?"

Elizabeth wasn't half wrong. Madoc had been hinting for months that Chalcedony should take Djamel or Tetrick for a mate. Her own father had been her mother's shadow. But she hadn't let her mind go there. It was too early for her to choose a mate. She wasn't going to torture herself until she had to.

"No, we are not secretly in love," Chalcedony said.

Elizabeth cut her deep caramel-colored eyes towards Chalcedony, looking as if she didn't believe her. "I can't find my tiara."

"Your what?" Chalcedony asked.

"My tiara." Elizabeth jumped from Chalcedony's arms. "I cannot be a princess without my tiara. It's what makes me special."

"I don't have a tiara, but I'm still a princess."

Elizabeth placed her hands on her hips and cocked an eyebrow. "Well, you're not doing it right."

"I don't know where your tiara is." Chalcedony was losing patience.

"Please! Please!" Elizabeth screamed, her waist-length hair swaying back and forth as she stomped her feet. "I can't be a princess without my tiara. Will you please help me look for it?"

Djamel stood and surveyed the room as if he was searching for something to attack. "What's wrong with her?"

"I don't know." When Coal had arrived from the human realm, he never screamed or cried. "Mireya!" Chalcedony shouted, almost as loud as Elizabeth.

Mireya ran into Chalcedony's room, wide-eyed and gasping for breath. "Princess, what is it?"

"Mireya, this is Elizabeth, the child I was telling you about." Chalcedony tried to speak over Elizabeth's cries.

"Well, you just about had my heart bursting out of my chest, Princess." Mireya faced Elizabeth. "Why are you crying, child?"

Elizabeth peered hatefully at the elf and began to cry again.

"Lizzy has lost her tiara." Chalcedony realized she would have to treat the child the way she treated an angry ambassador: pretend to care. "She can't be a proper princess without it. I think we left it in Coal's room. Please find it for her. It's a matter of life and death. Isn't it, Lizzy?"

Elizabeth stopped crying to answer the question. "Yeah, it's a matter of life and death. I can't be a princess without it."

"I'll get right to it." Mireya nodded to Chalcedony and walked out of the room.

Chalcedony faced Djamel. "We'll finish this tomorrow."

"Yes, Princess." Djamel bowed and left.

Tears stained Elizabeth's face. Chalcedony had never been allowed to cry as a child. "While Mireya looks for your tiara, let me share a secret with you."

"Okay," Elizabeth said, sniffling.

Chalcedony led the girl by her small hands to the portrait that hung across from Chalcedony's desk.

"This is my mother. She taught me that princesses never lose control. They never cry."

"Princesses cry all the time on TV."

"This isn't a movie. In real life, princesses who cry will not remain a princess for very long."

Elizabeth sniffled again. "Your mom is pretty. Why is she white and you're black?"

"I changed my skin color."

Her forehead crinkled as if she was trying to imagine something. "Why would you do that?"

"I liked this color."

"Can you change into my color?"

"Yes, if I wanted to."

"Oh. That's cool. Why is this sword here?" Elizabeth rubbed her hands over the glass case directly below the portrait.

"This was my mother's sword, Mayhem." Chalcedony gazed at the steel sword with its blue hilt. "It's a symbol of protection and strength. I used to beg my mother to let me play with it, even though I knew it was made just for her. If anyone else touched it, they'd die. One day, while the sword lay in its scabbard on my mother's bed, I touched it. Can you guess what happened?"

"You died?" Elizabeth giggled.

51

"Almost," Chalcedony said. "But before I passed out, Mayhem spoke to me. Just like I knew it would."

"What did it say?" Elizabeth leaned closer, suddenly serious.

Chalcedony shrugged. "I don't remember what it said, but it had spoken to me. That was all I cared about."

"But why did she need a sword? Aren't soldiers supposed to protect you?"

"Queens are more powerful than other fey. Once I'm queen, the power that has kept my abilities reined in will be released. I will be more powerful than twenty soldiers. My own sword will be my symbol of power."

"But princesses don't fight. They get rescued by princes."

"There are no princes here, Lizzy. We have to rescue ourselves or we die."

Elizabeth turned back towards the sword. "Is your mother dead?"

"Yes."

Elizabeth nodded. "Lots of princesses lose their parents on TV. I hope I never lose my mom."

"I'll never be able to do that." Coal anxiously watched Grigory recite incantations into a soldier's sword. It had only been a day since he'd accepted the apprenticeship, and already he felt overwhelmed.

Grigory straightened before he faced Coal. "What exactly are the rules about humans and magic?"

"Humans can't do magic, nor are we allowed to," Coal said automatically. That fact had been taught to him the moment he entered the fey realm.

"Has there ever been a moment you did magic in the entire time you were here?"

Coal hesitated. "One time." He'd promised Chalcedony he would never tell anyone. But other than Chalcedony, Grigory was the only person he trusted. Coal took a deep breath and continued. "Chalcedony has a secret portal out of Legacy. One day, Chalcedony found me moping in my room, and she asked me what was wrong. I told her I was sad because everyone treated me like I didn't belong, and that I wished I could do magic like her, maybe the others would be nice to me. She felt bad for me so she showed me her secret portal."

Coal waited for Grigory to speak. When he didn't, Coal continued.

"She said if I had a little bit of magic, even if it was as small as an apple seed, I could use her portal. Later that night, she taught me the spell, and we used it to travel into the forest."

"Did using the portal make you feel as if you belonged?"

"Others were still rude to me, but it helped. Knowing I had a little bit of magic made me feel as if I belonged."

Grigory grinned, making him appear ten years younger. "Magic as small as an apple seed."

"Excuse me?"

"If seeds are nurtured, they grow stronger and taller. Come over here," Grigory said. "There is no great secret to magic. Any fey would tell you that. But if you don't use it, how will it grow?" He took Coal's hand. "Do you feel anything in my hand?"

"It feels warm."

"What makes it warm? What makes your heart beat and your blood flow? What makes you move?"

Coal stayed silent, assuming the answer taught to him in school about the heart, blood, and proteins probably wasn't the response Grigory was looking for.

"Humans believe all things can be explained by science. But science can't explain why we are here. That is one of a few distinctions that separate humans from fey.

"Fey believe it is magic that makes our blood flow, our legs move, and in turn, makes some of us fly, some of us change colors, and some forge swords that equal no other. The beautiful chaos of the mind, magic, and soul cannot be explained. It can only be accepted and explored. The differences are as distinct and natural as blue or green eyes. For example, Princess Chalcedony tries her best to change the color of her eyes, but she can't. Some things are fluid, some aren't.

"Sit. Close your eyes. Think about what makes you walk, breathe, feel, love, weep. Find it. Bring it forth. It helps to have a focal point for the energy. Experiment. Use your hand or the center of your belly."

"Yes, Master."

Coal sat on the floor and closed his eyes, deciding to focus on his hand. He tried to recreate that small burst of energy he'd felt when he'd used Chalcedony's portal.

As time passed, his muscles ached with the desire to move, but he forced himself to remain still and concentrate. After what seemed like a lifetime, doubt outweighed his hope.

He opened his eyes. "I'm human. What if I don't have it?"

"If you didn't have it, you wouldn't be able to feel the sword or use it so well. You have it. You just don't know how to recognize it. Yet. That is enough for today. We'll practice more tomorrow. By the way, your room is ready. When do you plan to move out of Legacy?"

He hadn't thought about moving out. It made the change so official. "I'll start bringing my things tomorrow."

Grigory narrowed his brown eye. "Have you told Chalcedony that you've accepted my apprenticeship?"

"No." Telling her would really cement the decision. Once he told Chalcedony, there could be no turning back. "I'll tell her today."

"I'll see you tomorrow," Grigory said. "In the meantime, continue to nurture your apple seed."

Coal found Chalcedony in her room. Two blue tailored dresses lay on her bed. One dress was much smaller than the other. Chalcedony sat in front of her vanity mirror while Elizabeth ran a comb through Chalcedony's brown, wavy hair.

"What's going on? What are the dresses for?" Coal asked.

"Tell him, Lizzy," Chalcedony said, her voice full of anticipation.

"We're having a party." Elizabeth began jumping and clapping her hands.

"Why?" Coal asked. The child made the most ordinary things into monumental events.

"It was Lizzy's idea." Chalcedony had a smile just as wide as Elizabeth's. "Princesses are supposed to have lots of parties. I agreed because it'll give the staff practice for the coronation ceremony. Until then, we're keeping her in Legacy so everyone can meet her at the same time."

"And no boys allowed," Elizabeth added, wagging her finger at Coal.

"There will be boys. We can't have a party without Coal."

"Chaley, can I talk to you alone for a moment?" Coal asked, motioning to the hall with a nod of his head.

"Of course. Lizzy, I'll be right back." Chalcedony followed Coal into the hall.

"Grigory asked me to be his apprentice," Coal said, abruptly. "And I accepted."

"You're already there most of the time. I thought you were his apprentice already."

"He wants me full-time. I'm moving most of my things over there tomorrow."

She placed her hands on her hips. "You're leaving Legacy?"

"I've never heard of an apprenticeship being any other way."

"You can live here and do it. I'll talk to Grigory and work something out." She moved to leave, but he grabbed her arm.

"It's time for me to go, Chaley. Most fey my age have already left home for their apprenticeships. There are royal guards my age that have been on their own for years."

"They are not human. You are." Chalcedony clenched her jaw.

"I don't understand what the problem is, Chaley. You know I can't be here much longer. Madoc has threatened to kill me if I stay. The apprenticeship will keep me alive and in Everleaf," Coal said with frustration. The apprenticeship was a perfect solution. Why didn't she understand?

"But you will be leaving Legacy. You would be leaving me." She sounded wounded as if he wanted to hurt her.

"I'll be here. We'll still see each other," Coal whispered, his eyes darting around to make sure Madoc wasn't listening in.

"How can you be Grigory's full-time apprentice? You're human. You don't have magic. Sword making requires magic." Her eyes furrowed, the pain in her voice replaced with curiosity and doubt.

"He wouldn't have asked me if he didn't think I was able to do it."

"Maybe he feels sorry for you. Maybe he's just like Madoc and only wants you out of Legacy."

"Madoc wants me out of the fey realm, not just out of Legacy." If Grigory believed he had magic, that would have to be good enough.

Chalcedony stood straighter, her face expressionless. He'd seen her do that so many times over the years. It meant something had hurt her. He hated to see her hurt.

"I'm sorry, Chaley. But there's no other option."

"No," she said with a cold hard voice.

"What?" Coal asked, unable to believe what he'd just heard.

"No," she repeated, much softer. "It's too soon. Can you wait just a little longer?"

"He wants me now."

"He can't have you," she snapped, all softness gone. "You belong to me. You can't be out there walking around on your own. Anything could happen."

"Did you hear what you just said?"

That's the way she talked to strangers, to guards, or to her wait staff. That was not the way she talked to him. This should be the point where she lowered her head in shame and apologized. It never came.

Finally, Chalcedony spoke. "You can't leave yet. I still need you here."

"Sooner or later, I have to go, Chaley. It might as well be sooner." Heaviness grew in his chest.

"Tell Grigory I said no. End of discussion." To emphasize her point, she stomped away.

"You requested my presence, Princess," Madoc asked Chalcedony. She was sitting behind Legacy, playing with Lizzy. She had work to do, but she was playing as if she were a child again.

"You've been avoiding me all day."

"I didn't want to encroach on you and your new toy." He nodded towards the human child. The princess was regressing, and there was nothing he could do about it.

"Stop playing games. Say what you need to say and get it over with," Chalcedony ordered. Instead of facing him, she watched the child chase sprites. The small flying creatures had transparent wings like a dragonfly, and they darted from flower to flower.

"I said what I needed to say last night," he said.

"Coal told me you threatened to kill him if he stayed at Legacy."

Madoc chose his words carefully. "I did not threaten to kill him. I simply implied it. It's time for him to go. You know it. He knows it. The entire realm knows it. Let him go."

"He wants to move into Grigory's shop and become an official apprentice. I'm not letting him. Not yet."

"Why do you hang on to him?" Madoc asked, fighting to keep his voice steady.

She stood and faced him. "If Coal dies, I will kill you and whoever you get to do your dirty work."

She threatened his life as if she were ordering a servant to bring her a glass of water.

"Come on, Lizzy. It's getting dark, let's go inside." Chalcedony grabbed the child's hand and headed back into Legacy. Madoc was too old to fear death, but Chalcedony had never threatened his life. Good. The innocence she'd held onto so tightly was slipping out of her grasp. Perhaps there was hope for her after all.

"It's bedtime, Lizzy," Chalcedony said.

"I'm not sleepy."

Chalcedony stifled a yawn. "Well, I am. We've been playing all day."

"Will you show me some magic? Please, pretty please? Show me some magic, and I'll go to sleep."

"You promise?"

"I promise."

Chalcedony doubted she had the energy to do anything that would impress the child. She'd spent all day running around the yard, and answering endless questions Elizabeth had about the "fairy realm." The confrontations with Coal and Madoc hadn't been pleasant either. But she decided to do one of the first things she'd learned.

"Alright, watch this."

Elizabeth sat up, eyes wide. For the first time today, she was still and quiet. Chalcedony ran her fingers through Elizabeth's bone straight, black hair. A moment later, Chalcedony felt her own wavy hair straighten. She knew without looking that it was also darkening, becoming jet-black.

Elizabeth's jaw dropped. She shook her head, before standing on the bed and jumping. "Oh my god, oh my god, oh my god. You have hair just like mine."

Chalcedony sat on the side of the bed while Elizabeth's jumping shook her up and down. "You said you'd go to bed."

"I'm too excited to sleep. What else can you do? Will you change your skin color?"

Chalcedony shook her head and used the last amount of her energy to change her hair back to being wavy and brown.

Elizabeth groaned and stopped jumping.

"If you go to bed, I'll show you more magic tomorrow."

"Okay." Elizabeth yawned and lay down. "This has been so much fun."

"It has, but tomorrow you're going to sleep in your room," Chalcedony said absently. The guilt over her reaction to Coal leaving was bringing her mood down. After her mom had died, he'd been her everything. She needed to let him go, she knew that, but if he left, she would have lost everything that mattered to her.

"My room is scary. My mom always let me sneak into her bed. Daddy didn't like it though."

"I'm not a mom," Chalcedony said, trying to push aside thoughts of Coal.

"My mom always reads to me. Will you please read me a story?"

"You said you'd go to sleep if I showed you some magic."

Elizabeth stuck out her bottom lip and pleaded with her eyes. Despite Chalcedony's tiredness, she said, "Okay. I'll tell you one story and then, have to go to bed."

Tomorrow, she would apologize to Coal because she couldn't replace him. No one could. But he needed to give her time to get used to the idea. She'd apologize and he'd accept, just like always.

The muscles in his back and arms strained as he lifted the hammer and brought it down on the misshapen piece of metal.

Chalcedony almost forgot why she'd come as she watched his muscles ripple and contract with each swing.

In the middle of his fifth stroke, he stopped and his shoulders tensed. He knew she was there. But he lifted his hammer anyway, beating the metal with renewed urgency. The previous slow, rhythmic strokes were now chaotic and angry.

"Coal, I'm sorry!" Chalcedony shouted above the clang of the metal.

He put down his hammer, turned, and folded his arms across his chest. For a long moment, he stared at her. His intense gaze made her feel even guiltier.

"Did you hear me? I said I was sorry." She tried her best not to roll her eyes, or let any sign of impatience show on her face because she knew he'd drag her apology out longer if she did. He'd never given Chalcedony a free pass for being rude. Not even as children. She hadn't expected he would give her a pass now, but damn, did he have to draw it out? She'd said sorry.

He still remained silent. Was he really not going to forgive her?

Just as she was about to walk away, he spoke. "As long as we've known each other, you've never treated me like I didn't belong." The disappointment in his voice broke her heart.

"I didn't mean those words. I was shocked. I had no idea you were planning on leaving." She knew how other fey had treated him when he first arrived in the fey realm, so she'd tried everything she could to punish anyone who treated him badly.

"I don't know who you are anymore," he said as if he'd completely given up on her. "You're acting more like Madoc every day. I guess it was only a matter of time before you started treating me as if I didn't matter."

She stepped closer, fighting the urge to touch him. "You do matter. That's why I reacted so terribly. You've been a part of my life for so long that I don't know how to give you up." She bowed her head, too ashamed to meet his eyes. "I'm sorry. I was only trying to make you stay."

"I can do what I want and go anyplace I want, as long I have your permission?" he said calmly. "So I'm like one of your horses. Free to roam the fields, but that's it?"

"No, it's not like that. I've been selfish. I assumed you would be here forever." A shameful part of her wished she could keep him fenced, but then he really would hate her, and that would be worse than him leaving.

"What about when you have to find a mate?" he probed, sounding like he already knew the answer.

"Do you think I would let a pesky thing like a mate interfere with our friendship?" She tried to laugh, but it came out weak and desperate.

He closed the space between them, forcing her to stare into his eyes. *How could something so dark emit so much light?* "I've dreamed about our kiss every night since we got back." Coal said. He was so close she felt the heat emanating from his body, but he didn't touch her. It was an unwritten rule now.

He walked back to his anvil. "Madoc is right to separate us," Coal said with his back to her. He began to beat the metal again.

Dammit, her heart was about to burst out of her chest. But he stood steady and unapproachable. Damn him.

"How is my sword coming?" she hoped her voice was just as calm as his.

"You tell me."

He stopped working and walked into Grigory's shop. A moment later, he returned and handed her the sword. She had helped with the sword's initial design, but this was the first time she'd held it. The black leather hilt complemented the sleek double-edged steel. The pommel and the guard were golden and bright.

"It's beautiful!"

"Beauty is meaningless without a soul." His words were modest, but there was pride in his voice. "How does it feel?"

She'd never seen him like this. Bold enough to approach her about the kiss and now prideful. He wasn't only beginning to look like a man, but he was also growing into one.

"What do you mean by soul? How am I supposed to feel its soul?"

He picked up a sword lying next to the hearth. "Your sword loves to fight. Let's try it out."

She welcomed the opportunity to defeat him, and regain some of the power she'd lost by admitting she'd been wrong. Coal may be her best friend—she'd die for him—but she still hated to apologize.

"You've never been able to beat me in a fight. I don't want to embarrass you, in case your master returns."

Coal took a defensive stance and grinned. "We haven't sparred in a while, I may surprise you. Although you do have an unfair advantage because of your expertly forged sword."

Chalcedony mimicked his stance. "You may make the first move. I'll be gentle with you, I promise."

"No, ladies first. I pride myself on being chivalrous." Once again, he was the teasing, fun-loving boy she'd brought back from the human realm. "I'm waiting, Princess."

With each assault and counter already calculated, she attacked, releasing her frustration, embarrassment, and disappointment with every thrust and parry. She almost forgot—almost—that she was fighting against a friend, not a foe.

After a few attacks and counterattacks, she was breathing heavily and sweating. "You've gotten better. But …" she paused, "you're not good enough to defeat me." She quickened her thrusts, closing the distance between them and forcing him to retreat.

"How is the blade?" he asked after he successfully parried an advance.

"It's excellent. Well-balanced. It's a little heavier than my other sword, but I can get used to it. It's a perfect sword, but I don't feel its soul." Her voice was filled with disappointment.

"Are you sure?" he asked.

"It doesn't feel much different to the one I'm using now." She had hoped to feel the sensation she'd felt when she'd touched Mayhem as a child.

Coal stood still, looking confused. Chalcedony finally found the opening she had been looking for. She twisted away and hit him in the nose with her elbow. He fell onto the ground with a loud gasp.

"I win," she said, more tired than she wanted to admit.

"You are better with a sword than I remembered," he said as she helped him stand. "Are you sure you didn't feel anything from the sword?"

"It's a good sword, but I know what a sentient sword feels like. I held my mother's sword, remember?"

"Maybe you should name it."

Her eyes widened. "Yeah, like Mayhem." She tried to think of a name just as good as Mayhem. "How about Mischief?"

"I like it," he said, nodding his head in agreement. "Now you should carry it for a couple of days to make sure it handles right. The true bonding process may not take effect until the coronation, but I think having a name for it will help, too."

"Coal..." Chalcedony felt like a child. "Are we okay?"

He smiled as he stared into her eyes. "Of course we're okay."

"Will you wait until after the coronation to leave Legacy? It won't be the same without you."

Coal exhaled deeply. "When have I ever told you no?"

She wanted to touch him. "I'll see you back at home. And before I forget, the tailor has your clothes for the party. He needs you to come to his shop to make sure they fit."

"I already have something to wear."

Chalcedony placed a hand on her hip and tilted her head, mimicking Elizabeth. "I ordered something special for you."

He rolled his eyes. He hated dressing up, and he hated tailored clothes even more. "Yes, Princess."

She walked away both relieved and excited. He was staying at Legacy, and that was the first step in making sure he stayed permanently. Madoc and everyone else be damned.

CHAPTER SEVEN

The attic of Grigory's shop was small, cold, and drafty. It was nothing compared to his spacious room at Legacy.

He'd promised Chalcedony he wouldn't leave Legacy until after her coronation, but after spending most of the night trying to find his seed of magic, he'd decided to stay the night at the forge.

Sleep eluded him. The thought—and the hope—he could do magic had kept him up most of the night.

Despite last night's failure, Coal was anxious to try again. He sat cross-legged on the lumpy old bed, wrapped himself in a blanket to fight against the morning chill, and concentrated on nurturing his magic seed.

It was much easier to concentrate since Chalcedony had apologized. This argument had been worse than any of their other fights, and it had left him depressed and saddened. Now, everything was right in his world.

After spending hours trying to find his magic seed, Coal only managed to fall asleep and not wake up until morning. Giving up, he went to Legacy to deliver Djamel's repaired sword. He could've gone directly to the barracks, but he'd gone through the entrance, hoping to see Chalcedony.

"Good morning, Legacy." Coal rubbed the tree's bark.

It took a moment, but finally it said, *I guess it's a good morning. Where were you last night?*

"I stayed at Grigory's shop. Was anyone looking for me?"

No.

Coal had guessed right. Chalcedony would be too busy to notice he was gone. "Did you miss me, Legacy?" Coal asked, flattered. The tree was probably the only living thing that noticed he wasn't there last night.

It was the first time since you moved in that you were not here to say good night. I had hoped you'd moved permanently.

He was about to tell Legacy that he was trying to move out, but the sound of arguing drew his attention.

"Come here!" Mireya shouted. "Come here and take your bath."

"No," a shrill voice answered. "Leave me alone. I want to go home. I want my mom."

Coal walked towards the commotion. At the top of the stairs, a soaking wet Mireya was chasing Elizabeth in circles. "What's going on?" he asked.

As soon as he spoke, Elizabeth ran down the stairs and wrapped her arms around his waist.

"You come here." Mireya stomped towards them and pulled Elizabeth away, dragging Coal in the process.

"Hey." He held Mireya at arm's length, more to stop from falling over than to protect Elizabeth. "Calm down. What's going on?"

"I was told to give her a bath, but she keeps running away from me." Mireya's voice was filled with frustration.

"I don't want to take a bath. I want to go home."

A few days ago, Elizabeth hardly acknowledged he existed. Now, she clung to him like he was her only hope.

"I thought you liked it here, Lizzy."

"I want to go home. I want my mom!" she screeched.

"Why does she want to go home?" Coal asked Mireya.

"Because she's a child who needs her mother, Coal," she said as if the answer had been obvious. Mireya stepped closer and lowered her voice. "Of course she wanted to come. That doesn't mean she wants to stay."

"She poisoned me last night." Elizabeth pulled at his arm, interrupting Mireya.

Coal looked from Elizabeth to Mireya. "Is that true?" he asked.

"She had a hard time sleeping last night, so Chalcedony and I had a sleeping potion made for her. Of course, it didn't work. It just made her sick."

This time it was Mireya who pulled on his arm. "Will you take her for me?"

"But …" Coal stuttered, trying to think of a polite way to say no.

"Please. I need a break. Just for a few hours?"

"Sure. I'll take her for a little while."

"Thank you. Thank you." Mireya stomped away, leaving wet footprints in her wake.

Elizabeth stuck her tongue out towards Mireya and blew. Mireya returned the loud gesture before she continued out of sight.

"What did you do to her?" Coal asked.

"Nothing. She's just a mean, mean lady." Elizabeth frowned.

"Do you know when Chaley's coming back?" Coal asked. Maybe he could get rid of her sooner rather than later.

"No." Elizabeth pouted. "All she's been doing is working, and everyone else here is soooo mean to me. I don't have any friends, and I want to go home."

He remembered how some of the staff treated him when he'd arrived, and he instantly understood the child's grief. "Fine. Come with me. I'll bring you back to Chaley later."

He was beginning to wish he'd gone directly to the barracks. If Mireya couldn't control Elizabeth, how was he supposed to?

Coal left Legacy through the back entrance. It was late morning and recruits barely older than him were performing drills. They appeared nervous and excited, as Avonnah, Chalcedony's other shadow, shouted orders at them.

The smell of sweat and exhilaration was strong as Coal and Elizabeth walked past the new recruits and towards a group of wrestling fey.

"Why are those ladies fighting?" Elizabeth gripped his hand. He had to concentrate to not step on her.

"They're practicing to become better soldiers," Coal replied absently. He'd spotted Djamel in the cheering crowd surrounding the wrestlers.

"Hey, Djamel!" Coal shouted a few feet from the crowd. The shadow frowned, obviously not wanting to leave the fight. Once he saw Coal with his sword, his sour expression disappeared, and he tore himself away from the rowdy crowd.

"I've been getting my ass kicked without my lady by my side. The replacement you gave me was crap," said Djamel, and he took his sword.

"If the replacement was too good, you wouldn't want your original back."

Djamel shrugged and eyed Elizabeth. "Hello, Elizabeth." The shadow bent to one knee. "You look very elegant when you are not crying. But I can understand all of the fuss. The tiara looks good on you."

Elizabeth blushed and touched her tiara, never moving away from Coal's leg.

"Your charms are wasted on children, you know?" Coal said.

"Yes, but it never hurts to practice." Djamel winked at Elizabeth and stood. "I heard you are going to apprentice full-time with the half-breed."

"Yes." He was painfully used to Djamel and most of the soldiers calling the sword master a half-breed. However, they never called him that to his face.

"Good. I think Madoc was going to have me assassinate you if you stayed much longer."

Coal laughed hesitantly, wondering if Djamel was joking or telling the truth. Djamel took the flawed weapon from the sheath around his waist and gave it to Coal. He stepped back to swing his repaired weapon back and forth. "My lady feels good. Lizzy, do you mind if I use your escort for practice?"

"No," she said, barely above a whisper.

"It has to be quick. I have things to do," Coal said with apprehension, glancing down at the child at his side. Djamel stood with his feet in a slight lunge, sword lifted, eyes fixed on Coal. His expression changed from that of a charmer to a soldier.

Fear took root in Coal's belly. What if this was the opportunity Djamel was looking for? He could kill Coal and claim it was a training accident. Elizabeth tightened her grip on his hand.

"Lizzy," Coal said, "you have to step back so you don't get hurt."

She agreed and walked to the far side of the barracks. Coal took the replacement sword in his hands and mirrored Djamel.

"Don't look so scared, boy. I won't hurt the princess's—"

Coal didn't wait for him to finish. He stepped forward and swung at Djamel's head. Djamel met the high strike and hit Coal's sword away.

"Aye, boy. Give an elf a little warning before you try to behead him."

"How is the sword, Djamel?" Coal refused to let his guard down. "I have a job to do."

Djamel didn't answer. Instead, he stepped towards Coal and swung at the side of Coal's chest. Coal parried. Djamel, the quicker of the two, recovered and aimed his sword swiftly to the other side. By the time Coal realized Djamel's sword was no longer there, it was too late. Something sharp poked him in the abdomen.

It happened so fast, Coal didn't have time to be scared. He'd never fought Djamel, but he was sure his practicing with Grigory and almost defeating Chalcedony yesterday would let him hold his own against Djamel.

He had been wrong.

"You win," Coal admitted, glancing down at his stomach where Djamel had his sword's tip against Coal's stomach. It hadn't broken skin, but it was uncomfortable. Coal's heart pounded as he observed Djamel. The shadow's eyes were focused, intense, murderous. Perhaps Djamel had not been joking about Madoc's plan to have Coal killed.

Finally, Djamel lowered his sword. "The sword is excellent. But your talents are wasted as a swordsmith, human. You may have the makings of a great soldier instead."

Coal took a deep breath. "You just defeated me in less than five moves."

"Most don't get the chance to complete one move against me," Djamel said, before he walked back towards the wrestlers.

A soldier? Me?

Elizabeth pulled at his shirt, bringing him out of his thoughts.

"What are we going to do now?" she asked expectantly, with her dark eyes staring intently at him.

"Chaley hasn't taken you off the grounds, has she?"

Elizabeth shook her head. "She said no one in town is supposed to see me until the party."

He didn't want to go to the party, but he'd told Chalcedony he'd attend. That meant he needed to get his clothes from the tailor. "If you're coming with me, you'll need a disguise. I have a cloak in my room."

"You're too big. I can't fit any of your clothes."

"They're ever-changing clothes. They change to fit whoever wears them."

She gleamed. "Really?"

"Yes, really."

Elizabeth made some indecipherable sounds that Coal could only assume meant she was excited.

A few minutes later, they were on Coal's horse galloping away from Legacy and towards the town. Elizabeth sat in front with Coal's borrowed cloak hiding her face. His ever-changing pants that adjusted themselves to fit whoever wore them hid her short legs, but most wouldn't be fooled. They'd know she was human, but they wouldn't press to see her while she sat on a royal horse.

The cloak covered most of her face, but that didn't stop her from asking an endless string of questions about the fey realm and every single fey they passed. It wasn't until they passed a small elf and its mother that Elizabeth went eerily quiet.

He looked closer and saw tears trailing down her cheeks.

"What's wrong?" he asked, confused.

"I miss my mom." Elizabeth wiped away tears from her cheek.

"I thought you wanted to come and live here."

"I did, but now I'm ready to go home."

Coal remembered the distant, empty look on her mother's face before, and he gripped the reins tighter, his guilt resurfacing with the memory. "I'll talk to Chaley about it. Until then, you have to behave and listen to Mireya."

Elizabeth shrugged and remained silent.

"You have to promise me you'll be nice. She'll be nice to you if you're nice to her."

"Okay," she said softly. "I promise."

Chalcedony's feet dangled a foot above the floor as she sat in a giant chair mediating a meeting between giants and dwarves. The giants got to have the comfortable chairs while she and the dwarves had to climb up onto their chairs like small children.

"Those dwarves are using illegal human technology. There is no reason the metal content of our water should be so high. It tastes as if we are all drinking liquid steel!" Troysten, the giants' ambassador, shouted.

"Eh? We perfected our machinery centuries ago. We don't need human technology. It would only soil our work." The dwarf, Ambassador Eli, stood on his chair while he tried to outshout Troysten.

She'd had Madoc check the dwarves' method, and he hadn't found any human technology. There was no reason for the water to have changed. The giants insisted that the dwarves were behind the poisoning, and they were threatening war. But the dwarves were suffering just as much as the giants.

Mireya motioned to Chalcedony through a small opening in the door, bringing her from her thoughts. Chalcedony stood abruptly, eager for a reason to leave.

"Good fey, I have to go," she said, interrupting their argument. "Will you be at the party tonight?"

Ambassador Troysten scowled. "I have not finished, Princess."

"Ambassador, I searched the dwarves' mines and forges. They have not changed their operation. They are not polluting the waters. We will find out where this metal is coming from. Until then, we can only assume that it is naturally occurring."

"But—" Ambassador Troysten began.

Chalcedony continued. "I will form another group of both giants and dwarves. Natural or not, we will find the answer. So will I see you at the party?" Chalcedony insisted.

Troysten glared intensely at Chalcedony, but then nodded. "Fine. I'll see you at the party."

"Excellent," Chalcedony said, with an enthusiasm she didn't feel.

Mireya spoke as soon as Chalcedony left the conference room. "Princess, the guards have spotted Coal and the child. They have returned and are on their way to the stable."

Chalcedony was out of Legacy's entrance just as Coal and Elizabeth exited the stables. "Coal, where have you been?" she called. "You didn't take Lizzy into town, did you? I didn't want anyone to see her until the party."

"Do you want the truth or a lie?" he asked with a mocking grin. She crossed her arms over her chest and gave him a glare in response.

"I didn't have a choice." He shrugged. "Mireya and Lizzy were arguing like two dragons fighting over a piece of meat. Mireya begged me to take her."

"No one saw me. I was disguised," Elizabeth added, and turned a full circle in Coal's cloak.

"Don't worry," Coal said. "She was covered the entire time. No one in town got a good look at her."

He grabbed Chalcedony's arm and pulled her away from Elizabeth and Mireya.

"Coal, what are you doing?" Chalcedony's skin burned where his hand touched her and heat rose in her cheeks.

"Did you know she wants to go home?" he asked, releasing her arm.

"She's fine. She just had a hard time sleeping last night."

"Mireya said you were giving her sleeping potions that were making her sick."

"They think she's a magic null." Chalcedony admitted. "I had my most powerful magicians try to glamour her but nothing worked." Magic nulls were a myth, or so Chalcedony had thought. Any magic used on them didn't work. Not only could Elizabeth see through glamour, she was immune to it.

"Maybe she should go back home." Coal watched Elizabeth chase after some sprites.

"She'll get used to it here. You did."

He turned from Elizabeth and stared at her. His eyes were unreadable. "I didn't have a mother or a father. I didn't have anyone before you. You can't compare her to me."

He had a point, but she'd be damned if she was going to admit it. "She'll get used to it. We just need to give her some time."

"She asked me to take her home."

Chalcedony furrowed her brow. "And what did you tell her?"

"I promised her that if she didn't like it here after a couple of weeks, you and I would take her back."

"Really? You promised her that?"

"Yes."

Chalcedony rolled her eyes. "Fine. If she doesn't adjust soon we'll take her home. But look at her! She loves it here."

They both watched Elizabeth laugh and giggle while she chased after a couple of sprites. Elizabeth was having too much fun to leave, wasn't she? Coal was overreacting.

Chalcedony studied Coal while he studied the girl. Her thoughts spun. Maybe Lizzy was how she could get him to stay! Elizabeth seemed to like him better than Mireya. If Coal had someone to protect, it would keep him busy. Then, maybe, just maybe, Coal wouldn't leave.

Coal stood at Legacy's entrance and scanned the growing crowd. Chalcedony didn't have parties often, and he felt out of place among Everleaf's elite. He hoped the tailored cobalt-colored suit helped him blend in. Although he preferred to wear his hair in braids, he'd taken them down and was wearing a kinky afro.

Reds, oranges, and violets painted the horizon in thick, vivid streaks. Streamers and lanterns hung from Legacy's canopy, illuminating the section of the lawn reserved for the party.

All of the powerful households and ambassadors were there; even the waif, with both of its halves: one female and one male. They were hardly ever in the same realm together, and they were looking more solid than he'd ever seen them. Maybe having both parts of itself in the same realm helped.

Grigory stood next to one of a few dozen torches hanging from poles around the yard. He was watching the same dancers that had enthralled Coal a few nights ago. They didn't have the number of admirers they'd had at the market, probably because they weren't allowed to use magic on Legacy's grounds.

"I didn't expect to see you here tonight," Coal said to Grigory. The swordsmith was wearing light brown pants with a matching fitted shirt. His hair was combed back, showing his pointed ears. His beard had been shaved. It was the first time Coal had seen his mentor looking more like an elf than a dwarf.

"I received an invitation. It would have been rude to turn it down," Grigory said.

"I've never seen you do anything you didn't want to."

"I am the princess's to command. Just like every other member of her guard."

"She commanded you to come?"

"An invitation from the princess is as good as a command. You and Madoc are the only ones with enough clout to refuse her anything."

Hoping to guide the subject away from his perceived privilege, Coal said, "Chaley came to the shop yesterday and used her sword. She said it was beautiful and handled well."

"But?" Grigory asked, cocking his eyebrow over his one remaining eye.

"But she doesn't feel its presence. It handles like any other sword to her. How is it that I feel its soul but she doesn't?"

Grigory straightened. "They may not be compatible. Rejection doesn't happen often, but it isn't unheard of."

"If they've rejected each other, do you think we'll be able to have another sword ready by her coronation?" Coal asked, thinking of all of the work they'd put into forging it.

"It'll be hard, but doable. I'll need to see her with the sword to determine if they've truly rejected each other. What about you? Have you practiced anymore?"

Coal lowered his voice. "You mean practicing that thing that humans can't do and aren't allowed to do even if we could?"

"Yes."

"No," Coal lied. He'd practiced, but nothing happened. "I haven't had time."

Grigory began to speak but stopped mid-sentence.

"Grigory?" Coal asked before he followed Grigory's gaze. Elizabeth stood in the yard beside Chalcedony. Or at least he thought it was Chalcedony. She was wearing a blue dress that shimmered like a star whenever she moved. It was strapless with a gem-encrusted sash at the waist. As striking as the dress was, that was not the reason he stared. The person standing next to Elizabeth was Chalcedony's height and had Chalcedony's thin frame. But her skin was not dark. Instead it was beige, like caramel-tinted milk.

The crowd began a deafening, mind-numbing applause.

"Why would she do that to herself?" Coal asked, unable to hide his confusion and disappointment.

"What do you mean?" Grigory asked.

"She changed who she was—who she is."

"She only changed her skin color. Before she met you, she changed her appearance every day."

Grigory was right. It was only skin, only a color. But Coal couldn't help but feel jealous. He and Chalcedony had been a pair with their matching dark skin, and now she was paired with another.

"I'm going to get a drink," Coal muttered. In a few strides, he was at the table filled with five different types of wines.

On his third cup of apple wine, Queen Tasla stepped next to him and poured herself a glass. She had waist-length red hair that swayed whenever she moved. Her children, Tetrick, and Alisha, stood stoically behind her.

"Coal, you've grown much taller and more handsome since the last time I saw you." Queen Tasla ran her eyes over his entire body.

Coal bowed clumsily. "Thank you, Your Highness."

"Will you be changing your skin also?" Queen Tasla asked.

As usual, Tetrick treated Coal as if he didn't exist, but his sister, Alisha, stared at him with bright, mischievous eyes.

Coal returned her gaze, trying to figure out what she was thinking. "No, Your Highness. I don't have the ability to change my color," he said, answering Queen Tasla's question

"I'm sure one of Chalcedony's sorcerers could make you something," Alisha said. She had the same red hair as her mother's, but it was pulled back in a knot at the nape of her neck. Fresh scars, red and swollen, stood out from the front of her neck and disappeared down her dress.

"I like my color," Coal said.

"Humans have been known to kill over the color of their skin. So your species must think it's important." Queen Tasla walked back into the crowd with Tetrick trailing behind.

"You should come live with us. It seems like it may be getting crowded here," Alisha said.

"No," Coal replied. "I'm fine where I am."

He couldn't stop staring at her neck. Alisha noticed and trailed a finger along the scars. "My new beauty mark, thanks to a rogue troll in the human realm. Your princess will start collecting her own scars once Tetrick stops doing the dirty work for her."

She took her finger and touched Coal's lips. "Think about coming to our land. Your princess has replaced you. And by the heat emanating from you, it's obvious she hasn't been using you properly."

"Um," he stuttered. He wasn't sure if it was the wine or Alisha's touch, but his mouth went dry and his lips were on fire.

"Coal isn't going anywhere, Alisha." Chalcedony had moved across the room and was standing beside Coal.

Alisha leaned her head to one side and rolled her eyes. "You should share your toys, Chalcedony."

"He's not a toy."

"Alisha, stop teasing the boy. You are here as a shadow, not as a spoiled princess." It was Tetrick's voice, but he was nowhere in sight.

Alisha frowned and stepped back. "Yes, Tetrick." Her expression turned emotionless and focused before she disappeared.

Coal swallowed the lump in his throat. Chalcedony had changed, but not completely. Her intense red eyes were the same. Her scent—jasmine and vanilla—hadn't changed. Whatever it was that drew him to her, hadn't changed. She was still his Chaley.

"Your dress is beautiful," he said. Her blue gown caught the light, held it for a few seconds and returned it a few shades brighter.

She eyed him suspiciously. "Thank you. I thought maybe you'd be a little upset with me."

"Because of your skin color?" He shrugged. "I was, but as Grigory pointed out, you were never my color to begin with. Now that you're near me, I see that it doesn't matter. You're still the most beautiful person I know."

Chalcedony's cheeks turned crimson, something he'd never seen her do. He stepped closer and inhaled her perfume, before he whispered, "This color gives away your emotions."

"Coal, I think you've had too much wine." She backed away, cheeks blazing with fire. The sight warmed his heart even more than the wine. "There are fey watching. I …" she started, but a scream on the other side of the room drew her attention.

"No, I don't want to go with you!" Elizabeth struggled to pull her hand from Mireya. Chalcedony walked away from Coal, welcoming the distraction the little child provided. How much wine had he drunk?

"What's going on, Mireya?"

"She's falling asleep, but she refuses to go to bed," Mireya said.

"Let me go!" Elizabeth screamed.

"Lizzy, calm down," Chalcedony said, aware of the increasing crowd.

"I hate you!" Elizabeth screeched. "And I hate it here!"

"Let her go, Mireya. I'll take her." Chalcedony reached towards the struggling child while Mireya lifted her. In protest, Elizabeth kicked out, and her foot hit Chalcedony directly on the nose. The force and the pain sent Chalcedony falling to the floor. For a moment, Chalcedony forgot where she was. When the pain eased a bit, she forced herself back onto her feet and checked her nose. Her hand came away covered in blood. The room, which had been eerily quiet, buzzed with life again. A guard took Elizabeth from Mireya as a second guard aimed her sword at Elizabeth's neck. Coal appeared, standing between the armed guard and Elizabeth.

Chalcedony felt, more than saw, the entire guard draw their weapons.

"Stop!" Chalcedony screamed. A burst of pain exploded behind her eyes and the room began to spin. She never would have thought the girl kicked so hard. "Leave them alone."

"You heard the princess. Leave the girl alone," Coal said, with a combination of authority and relief.

Chalcedony scanned the crowd. They were all watching her. She ignored her throbbing nose and waved away the servants trying to help.

"But … she hurt you. She drew blood," mumbled the guard standing directly in front of Coal.

"Yes," Queen Tasla said. "She drew blood. You know what the law says."

Chalcedony wiped the blood from her nose onto the back of her hand. The dark substance contrasted sharply against her new pale skin.

"What do you know of our laws, Queen Tasla?" Chalcedony had only asked her to the party out of obligation, just as she did the other queens. Chalcedony hadn't expected or wanted her to come.

"I know enough to know that this particular law is the same throughout the realm." Queen Tasla gestured to Madoc. "Or have you not been taught your own laws?"

"She's right. Execution is required for anyone that draws the queen's or princess's blood," Madoc said as if he was reading a page out of a rulebook instead of condemning a child to death. "It is one of the first things the guards are taught."

"But she's only a child!" Coal exclaimed. He looked from Madoc to Chalcedony as if he was expecting Chalcedony to label Madoc a liar. But it wasn't a lie. It was one of the reasons the other children were not allowed to play with her as a child. Only royalty could hurt royalty. That law was one of the numerous reasons she'd brought Coal back with her from the human realm. She couldn't find a royal playmate, so she had to bring one back from the human realm. He hadn't known about the law because she'd forbidden anyone to tell him.

Thankfully, he'd never drawn any of her blood.

"The law makes no exception for age." Queen Tasla frowned. Chalcedony didn't let the queen's show of pity fool her. Tetrick's mother was not known for mercy.

"I know the law," Chalcedony growled. She may be forced to show the queen gratitude for allowing Tetrick to train her, but this was still her land, her home. Queen Tasla nodded and stepped back into the crowd, but Chalcedony felt the queen watching her, waiting for Chalcedony to make a mistake.

"Coal, take Lizzy to your room. The party is over. Everyone leave." Chalcedony forced herself to breathe through her swollen nose. She succeeded. Mostly. "Madoc, come with me."

CHAPTER EIGHT

"I didn't mean to kick her," Elizabeth cried, sitting next to Coal on the bed. "I just wanted to go home. Do you really think they're going to kill me?"

"No." He tried his best to sound reassuring. "Chaley knows it was an accident. She would never let anything like that happen to you."

"She doesn't like me anymore." Elizabeth sobbed. Her eyes were filled with tears, exhaustion, and fear. "I just want to go home."

A knock came from the door, and Elizabeth shrieked before she moved behind Coal and shielded herself. Mireya peeked through the slightly opened door as if she were looking for a threat. Satisfied with what she saw, she stepped through.

"Goodness, Coal. I'm so sorry. I had no idea the child would kick Chalcedony." Mireya clasped her hands in front of her face. When she stopped talking, she chewed anxiously on her thumbnails. "Do you really think they would execute a child?"

Elizabeth let out a muffled gasp and cried again.

"Oh!" Mireya cried in distress. "I didn't see her back there."

Mireya walked behind Coal and picked up Elizabeth. This time, Elizabeth didn't fight as Mireya reached for her. "Shh…" Mireya held Elizabeth against her breast. "Calm down. I'm sorry. Of course, they're not going to hurt you."

"Yes, they are. I hit a real princess. Not a fake one. A real one. They're going to hang me in front of an angry mob. That's what they do on TV."

"Shush, child. I've never heard of such a thing." Mireya laughed but the joy never reached her eyes.

"Will you stay with her?" Coal asked.

"Of course." Mireya rocked Elizabeth back and forth while she stroked the girl's hair.

"Thanks." Coal stood. "I need to talk to Chalcedony and find out what's going on."

"She's just a kid." Chalcedony had only requested Madoc, but, of course, every single ambassador—most had only come for free food—felt they had to give their opinion.

"The rule still applies. If anyone ever hurt you, they'd be executed. If Coal ever injured you, even as a small child, it would have applied to him," Madoc said. "You know the rules. You've always known the rules."

"They are waiting for you to slip so they can judge you weak. You were almost knocked unconscious by a human child. How much more weak can that be?" Troysten asked. The giant had to stoop in order to stand in the room. She'd chosen this room, hoping that at least he would be left out of the discussion. Of course, he wouldn't let a small thing like being uncomfortable keep him out. He was enjoying this. They all were.

The look on Queen Tasla's face still disturbed Chalcedony, like a cat waiting to pounce. She'd probably put Alisha in Chalcedony's place as soon as she found a way to do it legally.

"All the queens have agreed to leave Everleaf in peace until your coronation. But if you don't follow your own law and make an example of the child, they will not wait long before Everleaf is attacked," Ambassador Eli said.

Chalcedony was about to argue, but Coal stepped into the room. It was too much to have expected for him to stay in his room for the rest of the night.

"Coal, where is Lizzy?" Chalcedony asked.

"With Mireya," he answered.

"Why are you here?" Madoc asked. "This doesn't concern you."

Coal stiffened. "I brought Lizzy here to the fey realm. I'm just as responsible for her as Princess Chalcedony. Punish me, and let Elizabeth go home."

Madoc laughed. "That's so noble of you. I would never have thought you'd volunteer for execution."

Coal flinched, but stood firm, his back straight and chest out.

"We're not executing anyone, Madoc," Chalcedony remarked. If Madoc had his way, he'd execute Coal just for breathing.

"We could publicly whip her," Ambassador Eli said. "It's better than hanging."

"A whipping is not severe enough. Perhaps she should be sent to the weavers for a few years. She will be domesticated, if nothing else," Ambassador Troysten said.

"Yes," Ambassador Eli agreed, nodding his head. "Execution may be too harsh, but the weavers would be a fair punishment."

This morning, they were threatening to wage war on each other. Now, they were bonding over sending a human child to a labor camp? Madoc's Rule Number Five: A Common Enemy Will Make Two Foes Friends.

Coal raised his voice over the murmurs of agreement. "You cannot do that. The weavers work adult fey within an inch of their lives. How would a child possibly survive?"

"She would live. There are potions and magic to ensure she stays alive," Ambassador Troysten said.

"She is a magic null. None of those things will work on her."

"Yes," the head sorcerer said with a mouthful of cake he'd brought from the party. "I have never seen one of those. Perhaps you can donate her to me for experiments?"

"Chaley, you can't let them—" Coal said.

"Boy, silence!" Madoc shouted. "You have no say in this matter."

"Coal, please leave, and make sure Lizzy is okay." Chalcedony passed a weary hand over her eyes. Her nose still throbbed and she couldn't wait to get out of her damn dress.

"You want her to sleep now so she can be well rested to be tortured tomorrow?" Coal snapped.

"Boy, you're stepping outside of your role as the princess's toy." Madoc's words were flat and calm, but Chalcedony heard the threat laced in them.

"Coal," Chalcedony ordered. "Leave."

"Can I speak to you in the hall?" Coal held her gaze, pleading with his eyes.

Madoc spoke up. "Princess, we need to—"

"I'll be right back," she said, interrupting Madoc before she followed Coal into the hall. If she didn't go with Coal, she'd have two human lives to protect instead of one.

Once they were in the hall and the door was closed, he grasped her chin and studied her face. "How is your nose?" Wine lingered on his breath.

Despite everything, she couldn't help but be flattered by his attention. "I feel like I'm speaking underwater. Other than that, I'm fine." Feeling herself blushing, she stepped back, hoping the distance would quench some of the heat. "Is that why you called me out here?"

"You promised me that if Lizzy didn't like it here we'd take her home."

"That was before she assaulted me. The law supersedes that promise."

"Damn the laws! You are going to be queen. You dictate the law, not your advisors, and especially not Madoc."

"He only wants the best for Everleaf. If I am weak, we all pay."

"Madoc is determined to turn you into a monster."

"He is training me to be a queen."

"To him, a monster is no different than a queen."

"You don't know what it's like out there. My name protects you."

"Let me see what the world is like without your protection."

Chalcedony clenched her fist. "Why do you want to break my heart?" How had they gotten onto this subject again?

"Because every day with you is breaking mine. Chaley, please let me go. Allow me to take Lizzy back to her family."

She tried to think of the perfect rebuttal—the solution that would solve all of their problems. Unable to think of anything, she walked towards the door. "You are free."

"What about Lizzy?" Coal asked.

"I was naive to think anyone could replace you." She fought the urge to reach for his hand. "Now, Lizzy will have to pay for my mistake."

"Chalcedony."

"Go away." She'd always tried to keep her duties separate from her relationship with Coal. Now, they were coming to a disastrous head. "If you stay any longer, they will expect your life for disrespecting me." He didn't move. Chalcedony saw him searching for something to say to change her mind. "There is nothing more you can do for her. Leave, or I'll have you sent away."

He didn't listen. He was right behind her when she stepped back into the room. "Djamel, take Coal to his room and make sure he stays there for the rest of the night."

"Yes, Princess." Djamel was instantly at Coal's side.

Why hadn't Djamel been so quick when I was getting kicked in the face?

"Chaley!" Coal shouted. "Don't do this. We can take her home!"

"The noise, Djamel," Chalcedony said.

Djamel covered Coal's mouth with his hand and dragged him from the room.

"Just let me talk to them. I can make them understand," Coal pleaded after being shoved into his room.

"You're not going to make them do anything, little man. You are only making it worse. Stay out of it. Let Princess Chalcedony take care of this."

"Djamel …" Coal tried to push past, but he found himself lying on the floor holding his cheek before he even realized he'd been hit.

84

"I'm finished talking." His face hardened into something unrelenting. "Shut up, and go to sleep. Or do you want me to put you to sleep?"

Coal's eyes teared up from pain. He wiped them before he righted himself.

Djamel's voice softened as he spoke to Mireya and Elizabeth. They were holding each other as they sat shivering on the bed. They'd watched the whole thing in silence. "Sorry about that, Miss Elizabeth and Mireya. I didn't mean to scare you."

Mireya nodded, before Djamel walked out of the room and closed the door. Cowardice won out over Coal's desire to leave. Reluctantly, he stood. "Mireya, you can go."

"I'm so sorry. I had no idea she would kick Chalcedony. I swear I didn't."

"It's okay." Coal rubbed his cheek. "I'll sit with Elizabeth until morning."

Mireya kissed Elizabeth on the forehead before she approached Coal. She said in a hushed tone, almost whispering, "I'm sorry. The child and I weren't getting along. I should have had Chalcedony find another caretaker."

Coal shrugged. It was done and over with now. They couldn't change what happened, no matter how much they wanted to.

"Did you talk to Chalcedony? What are they going to do?"

Coal stayed silent.

"It was that bad?"

"Yes," Coal admitted.

"She told me you were going to take her home. If Chalcedony was going to let anyone do it, it would be you."

"But—" Coal said.

"Hush, boy. Don't argue with me. Did you promise to take her home?" Mireya asked.

"Yeah, but—"

"No buts. Keep your promise."

"What am I supposed to do? Chalcedony isn't listening to me," Coal said, despair weighing heavy on his chest.

"You do whatever it takes," she ordered before she knocked on the door. Djamel opened it, and she was gone. Coal watched the door, too ashamed to face Elizabeth.

"Are they going to kill me?" Elizabeth asked, filling the silence.

He faced her and tried to sound cheerful. "No. They were just trying to scare you. Everything will be better in the morning."

"Can I go home tomorrow?"

"Maybe. If you go directly to sleep." The lie cut at his heart. But what did it matter? She'd be gone tomorrow, and he'd never see her again.

"Okay. I'll be good." She wiped her nose on the back of her hand before she clenched her eyes and feigned sleep.

As he paced the room, he kicked a small bottle across the floor. After he picked it up, he realized it was the sleeping potion Mireya had told him didn't work on Elizabeth. His heart quickened as he stared at the small bottle in his hand. Had Mireya left it on purpose? She'd already told him it didn't work on Elizabeth, but it could work on others …

Do whatever it takes to keep your promise.

Before he lost his nerve, he knocked on the door and pulled off the black stopper of the potion.

Djamel opened the door with a hand on his sword. "What is it?"

Coal brought the bottle up to his mouth and blew. As soon as the dust hit Djamel's face, his eyelids closed and he fell backward. Coal grabbed Djamel's shirt and pulled him into the room before he hit the floor. It took all Coal's strength to pull the unconscious fey onto the bed, before he ran to the door and closed it.

Elizabeth stood in the corner of the room shaking. "Is he dead?"

"No," Coal replied, shocked by the question. "I just used some of your sleeping potion on him."

She cried as if she didn't believe him and thought she would be next.

"I promise. He's not dead," Coal said. "See? His chest is moving. He's breathing."

Elizabeth walked slowly over to Djamel's motionless body. "Oh."

"Lizzy, do you really want to go back home?"

"Yes," she whispered as if she was scared to wake up Djamel.

"Then, you have to trust me. You can't cry. You've seen Chaley. Princesses are strong. They don't cry, and they don't hesitate."

"I don't want to be a princess anymore. I just want my momma." She began crying again.

"Princess or not, you do not get to cry. No crying until you get home. Do you understand me?"

She stopped sobbing, but her lips quivered.

"If you want to go home, you can't cry," Coal said. "You have to be brave."

"Like a soldier?"

"Yes, be a soldier. You have to promise to do what I say, or you won't make it back to your mom."

"I'll be brave. I promise," she said, sounding more confident.

"Good, let's go."

He covered her in the cloak she had worn earlier and carried her out of his room.

Coal's heart pounded in his ears as he and Elizabeth hurried to Chalcedony's room. They'd been lucky. The hall and the stairs were empty. Everyone was either in the conference room discussing Elizabeth's punishment or cleaning the mess from the party.

He put Elizabeth down in front of Chalcedony's door and motioned for Elizabeth to stay quiet by placing his index finger on his lips. She nodded.

"Chaley," he whispered, praying no one would answer. Magic guarded the door, and Madoc, Coal, Chalcedony's shadows, and now Elizabeth were the only ones allowed to enter the room. If an intruder entered, Legacy would alert Chalcedony and Madoc.

When no one answered, Coal turned the doorknob. He was about to enter, when Elizabeth pulled him back.

"No," she whispered, fresh tears glistening in her eyes.

He bent down and tried to put as much urgency in his voice as he could while still whispering. "The way out of Legacy is through Chaley's room. You don't have to be afraid. She's not in there. It's empty."

Elizabeth didn't look reassured. She held his hand so tight it was going numb, but when he stood and entered the room, she followed.

The moonlight beamed through the window, highlighting the dressing screen. It almost felt like an omen, Coal thought as he walked further into the room.

"Are we climbing out of the window?" Elizabeth asked.

"No, there is a magic portal behind the screen."

"Oh," Elizabeth said, making it sound like a question.

He stopped when he saw Mischief sheathed on the bed. The sight made his hand itch. What if Bren had disobeyed Chalcedony's order and still patrolled the forest?

With the sword strapped to his back, they continued to the back of the screen. He'd return it as soon as Elizabeth was back home, he promised himself.

Elizabeth moved closer as they huddled together in the cramped space. Moonlight spilled over the top, giving them enough light to see.

"How does it work?" Elizabeth whispered.

"I say the spell, and then we'll be magically transported to the forest."

"But we're human. You said humans can't do magic."

"According to Chaley, the door holds most of the magic. If I can do a little magic, the screen should do the rest."

He didn't tell her about how Chalcedony had made him promise not to use it. Chalcedony would understand, he reassured himself. She'd be mad at first, but he was giving her a way out of punishing Elizabeth. Instead of her looking weak, he'd be the traitor—the human gone bad. That's what they'd always expected from him anyway.

"Are you ready?"

Elizabeth nodded.

Coal closed his eyes and recited the simple verse Chalcedony had taught him when they were young. "Take me from this place. Take me to the forest. Let me run. Let me be free."

CHAPTER NINE

Coal opened his eyes, expecting grass underneath his feet, but Legacy's wooden floor was still beneath him. He bit his lip. Elizabeth stood with her eyes closed so tight it seemed as if she were steeling herself against getting hit.

I must've said it wrong. He began the verse again. This time he kept his eyes opened and enunciated each syllable of the spell.

Nothing happened.

Elizabeth opened her eyes. "Are we almost there?"

"One more time," he said, with false cheerfulness.

He repeated the spell.

Once again, nothing happened.

Maybe she'd moved the door or changed the spell. But she'd told him it had been the same for generations. *What am I doing wrong?* he thought frantically.

Then he remembered. The first time he'd used the portal, Chalcedony had said the rhyme quietly with him. He'd thought it was strange at the time, but he'd dismissed it as Chalcedony making sure he'd said the spell right. He had been so eager to believe he had magic that he'd ignored the fact she'd also been saying the spell.

Chalcedony had made the door work, not him, he realized. She'd told him that anyone with a little bit of magic could open it and he'd believed her. His heart ached as he admitted to himself that he had no other plan to get Elizabeth past the guards.

"Lizzy, it's not working. I'll have to think of some other way to get us out."

"What's wrong with it?" she asked.

"I thought I had enough magic to make it work, but I don't."

"Maybe I do," she whispered.

"We can't do it because we're humans. I'll think of something else. There has to be another—" He stopped short when he heard something outside Chalcedony's door.

"Someone's coming." He wasn't sure what Chalcedony would do if she found them there, but once they found Djamel passed out in his room, there was no way he could pretend he wasn't trying to escape with Elizabeth.

He looked down to check on Elizabeth, when he heard her reciting the spell.

"We're human, it won't work," he said, just before the world disappeared and the force of something invisible and dark took his breath away.

After a few horror-filled heartbeats, the world reappeared under Coal's feet. Unable to keep his balance, he fell to his knees. His heart beat as if it were going to explode. His head hurt. It was as if he'd been ripped out of Legacy and a little piece of his brain had remained behind. For longer than he would have thought possible, his world was nothing but pain and chaos. He pulled at something—the wet grass—as a bout of pain shot through his head. Slowly, the worst of the pain passed.

He had been holding hands with a little girl—Lizzy.

He opened his eyes. The moon, although bright, only showed the silhouette of wildflowers and trees. "Lizzy," he muttered, "where are you?"

Something groaned in the distance.

"Lizzy!" On his hands and knees, he tried to determine the direction of the moan. His head felt like it was about to burst. What had happened to him? This hadn't happened when he'd used the portal with Chalcedony. What if he had hurt Elizabeth? He stood, trying his best to ignore the searing pain.

"Lizzy, where are you?"

"Ahhh," Elizabeth moaned.

Searching, he saw her black cloak lying a few yards away. He half-ran, half-stumbled towards her.

"Are you okay?"

"That was fun." She giggled.

He pushed her away. "You scared me."

She stood, laughing. "That was so much fun!"

Coal grabbed his head; her laughter made his headache worse.

"Are you okay?" she asked.

He took his hands from his head and opened his eyes. "I'm okay. How are you?"

"I'm fine." She jumped up and down. "Did I do magic? I did magic, didn't I?" Her face glowed in the moonlight. The brightness hurt his eyes and he had to look away.

"I don't know if you did magic." Why was his head hurting? He assumed it was from the portal, but if so, why wasn't Elizabeth in pain?

"Then why didn't it work with you?"

"I don't know." His head hurt too much to think of an answer. He didn't care. He should have cared, but he didn't. "What are we doing in the middle of the forest? We should go back home to Chaley."

Her smile disappeared. She dimmed, almost blending into the darkness once again. "No. You promised to take me back home."

"Take you back home?" he repeated. Then, he remembered why they were there. How had he forgotten? He breathed deeply and the world became less foggy. "Yes, I'll take you home, and then I can return to Legacy. That's the plan."

"Okay." She clung to his hand. "Which way do we go?"

"Princess," Avonnah said through Chalcedony's door.

Chalcedony moaned and peered outside her window. The sun was still low in the sky in an early, dark-blue dawn. "Go away. I'm sleeping!"

"B-b-but—" Avonnah stuttered. "It's important."

"You heard me. Go away."

There was always something important. Urgent matters that couldn't wait, but she needed sleep. Staying up half of the night listening to the dwarves and the giants argue about the punishment of a little girl had been draining. However, by the end of the night, they had bonded and agreed to work together on their water problem.

Now, she deserved some rest.

Just as she had managed to fall back to sleep, Madoc's voice boomed through the door. "Wake up, Chalcedony."

"It's early. Let me sleep. Can't you wait one more hour until you have me send a little girl to be worked to death?"

"They're gone."

Chalcedony lifted her head from her pillow, heart racing. "Who's gone?"

"Coal and the child," Madoc answered. "They've run away."

She jumped out of bed, almost tripping on the blanket wrapped around her foot. She threw open the door. *Run away? Coal and Elizabeth?* "That's impossible. Djamel is guarding them."

"He was knocked out by the sleeping potion that was supposed to be used on the girl."

Her thoughts were racing, but she asked coolly, "How long have they been missing?"

"No one noticed Djamel was gone until five minutes ago."

Coal would never run away. She had given him permission to lead his own life, yes. But he would never leave without saying goodbye. "I assume you've already locked down Legacy and you're searching the town?"

"Of course," Madoc said.

Dammit. Dammit. Dammit. She fought the urge to place her hands in her hair and let everything soak in a bit longer, but hesitation was not part of her training. "Is Djamel still in Coal's room?"

"Yes. He's having a hard time recovering from the sleeping potion."

She walked past Madoc and Avonnah and headed for Coal's room. Madoc's Rule Number Ten: See It For Yourself. Only Rely On Second-Hand Information If You Have No Other Choice.

Djamel sat on Coal's bed, cradling his head.

"Djamel, what happened?"

He saw her and quickly averted his eyes. She didn't know if it was because she was wearing her nightclothes, a bra, and panties, or he was ashamed for letting a human boy outmaneuver him. With as many ladies as Djamel was rumored to court, it was probably the latter.

"Talk," Chalcedony ordered.

"Yes, Princess." He kept his gaze on the floor. "Coal knocked on the door, I opened it, and then he blew something in my face. The next thing I know I'm being doused with water."

She made herself stand completely still, watching for any movement from Djamel that might indicate he was lying. "What time were you knocked out?"

He closed his eyes as if to concentrate. "Not long after I was ordered to his room."

"Are you sure no one took them? We had a lot of guests last night."

"It was Coal who blew the potion at me. No one else was in the room except for the girl."

"Legacy's protective spells would have alerted us if anyone had tried to take them by force," Madoc added.

She bit her lip. "Where the hell would they go?" she said, more to herself than anyone else.

But Djamel answered, "He seemed intent on getting that girl home."

"Avonnah, did anyone see them leave?"

"They didn't leave through any of the main entrances. The guards were adamant about that."

"Damn him." There was only one other way out. "Damn him!"

"Get up, Djamel," Chalcedony crossed her arms and tilted her head. "You had a very simple task: keep Coal in his room."

"I know, Princess. I failed."

"Avonnah, you were just promoted." Chalcedony never took her gaze from Djamel. "Give her your sword."

He grimaced, but then straightened his face just as quickly. It wasn't much, but demoting him made her feel a little better.

"Avonnah, get a group of guards together and meet me in my room," Chalcedony ordered before she left.

Damn him! Coal was such an idiot. She should have known he was going to do something like this. She understood him trying to protect the girl out of his overblown sense of morality. But betray her? He would never do that. There had to be some other explanation.

"Are we almost there?" Elizabeth asked with a low, nervous voice. The only sound in the forest was the shuffling of their feet and chirping crickets. It was still dark, but the sun had begun peeking from behind the horizon.

"Yes." He hoped she didn't hear the doubt in his voice. They'd been walking all night and they should have run into the door by now. When he'd come with Chalcedony it had been daytime. The darkness made him doubt himself.

"Your hand is sweaty," Elizabeth said.

Coal laughed. A little while ago, it had been her hand that was sweaty. "I'm a little hot."

"But it's cold out here."

Coal shrugged. Maybe he wasn't hot. Maybe he was cold. "We have to hurry. We still have far to go."

"You said we were almost there."

"We'll be there soon," he said sharply. He didn't want to answer any more questions. Time was no longer making sense. His eyelids felt as if they weighed a ton, and his feet dragged. Every movement took all of his strength. He should have stayed at Legacy.

"Are you okay?" Elizabeth asked.

"I'm fine," he lied. "We're almost there."

"How can you tell? Your eyes are closed."

"No, they aren't." He forced his eyes open. The effort made him fall to the ground. "Just let me rest for a little while."

"Get up. We don't have time to rest. Let's go." She pulled his arm, groaning with the effort.

"I'm up." Coal made it to his knees. His head hurt. His entire body hurt. A small, cool hand touched his forehead.

"You're hot," Elizabeth said. "What's wrong with you?"

"Nothing is wrong with me." He tried to stand, but fell and everything began to spin. *Am I dying? I can't die out here. Who will take Lizzy home if I die?* "Come on. We have to go back."

"No. You said we can't."

"We have to. We don't belong here." He became stronger just saying the words. He grabbed Elizabeth and began dragging her, his strength finally returning. It felt good to feel good.

"No," Elizabeth said. "I don't want to."

"We have to go back." Coal tightened his grip on her arm. She clawed at his hand, digging her nails into his skin. He ignored the small stabs of pain and pulled. "We have to go back."

CHAPTER TEN

Chalcedony knelt in the forest and placed her hand in the grass. Concentrating, she ignored the early springtime chill and focused on sensing Coal. She'd never tried to find someone by feeling for their presence, but she knew Coal better than anyone. She knew when he entered the room. She knew when he was happy. She knew when he was upset. And she had always been able to sense where he was in Legacy.

If he was here, she knew she'd be able to feel him.

She didn't. So he wasn't. But he had been.

He'd lain right here in the grass. Where the hell was he now? She stood and wiped her damp hands on her thick leather pants. Neither Coal nor Elizabeth should have been able to make it out of the forest. Why couldn't she find them?

The six soldiers she'd brought through her once-secret portal stared expectantly while they waited for orders.

"Search the forest again. They have to be here somewhere." She knew they weren't, but that was the only order she could give until they learned something new.

"Are you sure they're here, Princess?" Madoc asked. So far, he had been calm through the whole ordeal, but his passivity meant nothing. This is what he'd been warning her about. This is what he had been expecting.

"His trail leads here. This is where he rested."

"Are you sure?"

"Stop asking me stupid questions. Of course, I'm sure. He's trying to take her back to the human realm. You saw their trail as clearly as I did."

Why the hell did it disappear?

She wanted to believe they had been kidnapped. But only Coal, in his ignorance, would have thought this was the way to the human realm. She was stupid to have trusted him, stupid to have shown him the way there.

"They shouldn't have made it this far. Someone is hiding them."

"Who would risk punishment to help him?" Madoc asked.

"I only know of one person who would do that."

She headed back to Legacy.

Madoc grinned as he watched Everleaf's future queen stalk away. Suddenly, he was happy he hadn't had the boy killed. Common sense had told him to get rid of the boy long ago, but the prophets had told him to keep the boy around, despite the gossip and the princess's failure to mature as he'd hoped. But within the past hour, she'd matured exponentially. Overnight, she'd become determined, calculated, and focused.

He had no idea how this was going to play out. Chalcedony was right. The boy shouldn't have been able to make it this far. The admission made him more than a little bit uncomfortable. He hadn't been in a situation where he didn't know the outcome since before Chalcedony's mother died. Knowing the end of everything made life dull. These were the moments he lived for.

Coal woke feeling as if he'd overslept and was late again for apprenticing with Grigory. However, when his eyes focused on a dirt ceiling in a dimly lit room, he knew he wasn't home.

His heart quickened as he remembered running away with Elizabeth to take her home. A wave of defeat passed over him. He'd failed. This dark, dank room was probably an underground cell at a labor camp. Was Elizabeth here, too? Or had he made it worse and she'd already been executed?

Through the flickering light of a candle hanging across the room, Coal saw that Mischief and his cloak were lying on the table next to him.

The door opened. Coal instinctively grabbed the sword and pointed it towards the opening. He was sure there were guards everywhere, but if they were stupid enough to leave his sword, maybe he had a small chance of fighting his way out.

A blonde female dwarf with light-blue eyes walked into the room.

"Who are you?" he asked, looking past the dwarf, expecting someone bigger and scarier. "Where is Lizzy?"

She cocked an eyebrow while she glared at his sword. "It's impolite to point."

"Where is Lizzy?" He gripped the sword tighter, taking comfort in the familiar metal, which was, as usual, anxious for a fight.

"Please don't point your sword at me," she said with a clenched jaw.

"I won't hurt you if you tell me where Lizzy is."

She ducked under the sword and then appeared on his other side. "I told you to put the sword down." She jumped and hit him in the chest with her fist.

His heart skipped a beat, and then another, making it impossible for him to breathe or think coherently. As he struggled to breathe, he saw the dwarf step back and run towards him. Before he could move out of the way, she rammed into his stomach, knocking him over. The last thing he felt was something hard hitting the back of his head.

"Coal, are you awake?" Something jostled him. "Wake up. It's time to eat."

Coal sat up quickly, heart racing and his hand clutching his chest.

"Lizzy, are you okay?" he asked in a hurried voice. "Did that dwarf hurt you?" His eyes darted back and forth as he searched the room for the small blonde.

"Why would Haline hurt me?" Elizabeth asked. Her dress from the party had been replaced by a long black shirt tied at the waist with a leather belt. "Haline said it's time for you to wake up. You've been asleep for a long time."

"Who is Haline?" He stood and rubbed the bump on the back of his head. "Are we at the labor camp?"

"No, we're at Haline's house." Elizabeth's tone suggested that Coal was supposed to have known the answer already.

"Where is my sword?"

"I don't know. Let's go. I'm starving." She tugged at his arm.

"No. It's not safe. That dwarf is dangerous." Coal suppressed the urge to rub the bump on the back of his head once again. "We have to get out of here."

"I'm an itty bitty dwarf." Coal recognized the sultry voice of the fey that had knocked him unconscious. "How dangerous can I be?"

He pulled Elizabeth behind him. "Where is my sword? We're getting out of here."

"The girl is obviously safe." Haline's voice remained calm and innocent as if she hadn't attacked him.

Elizabeth ducked under Coal's arm and ran to Haline. "Stop being mean. She's helping us."

The dwarf and Elizabeth were the same height. Haline stared at Coal with frigid blue eyes, before she winked and faced Elizabeth. "I'm starving, Lizzy. Let's go eat."

Elizabeth bit her lip, looking anxiously from Haline to Coal. "Are you coming? I promise she's nice."

Whoever the dwarf was, she had completely fooled Elizabeth. "Give me my sword back if you're not going to harm us," he ordered.

"You attacked me. You'll get it back when you leave. House rules," Haline said, before she left the room. Elizabeth hesitated for a moment before she followed.

Coal rubbed his flattened afro as he tried to figure out what had just happened. Before he could think of any answers, he smelled something delicious. The aroma reminded him he hadn't eaten since this morning.

Elizabeth beamed with joy when Coal sat in the small chair at the dwarf-sized table. Apparently, they had been expecting him because there was already a bowl full of something hot and steaming sitting in front of him.

"It's rabbit stew." Elizabeth dipped a spoon into her bowl and slurped. "I helped Haline skin it while you were asleep."

Elizabeth's joy was infectious. Then he recalled getting hit in the chest. He needed answers before he ate. He gazed towards the dwarf. "Where are we?"

"In my home."

"Underground?"

"Yes." Elizabeth answered for Haline, nearly bouncing out of her chair. "I've never been in an underground house. It's so cool."

"How did we get here?"

Elizabeth's excitement disappeared. She stared at her stew as if she'd lost a tiara in it.

Haline placed her spoon beside her bowl. "I found the girl crying in the woods while you were forcing her back to Legacy. It was obvious she didn't want to go, so I shot you with a poisoned dart and dragged you here."

"What do you mean I was trying to drag her to Legacy? I was sick, I remember that, but I was trying to take her to …" Coal shifted in his too-small seat. "… Legacy. Then you know who we are?"

"How many humans do you think get lost in these woods? Of course, I know who you are: the queenling's toys. Although I heard she don't much care for the girl."

He stared at his bowl, moving the chunks of meat and carrots around in a circle. His appetite had disappeared. "Are you going to turn us in?"

"I don't like you, but I like the girl. I'd hate to see her go to the weavers."

Haline leaned towards Coal and whispered, "But why give up your life of luxury for this child? If you return her, the princess would forgive you. It's no secret she loves you."

My life of luxury? Did the entire realm think he was coddled and spoiled? "I promised Lizzy I'd take her home. I just didn't know I would get sick."

"You weren't sick. You were hexed."

He laughed uncomfortably. "I would know if I had been under a spell. I was just sick."

"The spell was meant to make you ill if you ever ran away. You're lucky I had the counter spell and potions needed to reverse it."

He'd heard of similar spells being cast on children and wandering spouses. Coal shifted in his chair as he recalled the intense desire he'd felt to return to Legacy.

"I've been away from Legacy before, and I've never been sick."

"There is a difference between being away and running away."

"I was coming back as soon as Lizzy was back in the human realm."

"If you truly believed that, you wouldn't have gotten sick. By the way, how were you going to get her home?" Haline started eating again.

He didn't know if he should trust her, but he didn't have any choice. "I was taking her to the door for the human realm. We were almost there. I just couldn't find it before I got sick." He suppressed a groan as he thought about all the trouble he had gotten them in for nothing. "The door is probably guarded now. I'll never be able to get her through it."

"There ain't a door there," Haline said with a mouth full of meat.

"Yes, there is. That's how Lizzy got here."

Haline shook her head as she rolled her eyes. "Not anymore. It moved."

"How is that possible? Chalcedony would have told me if it moved."

"Just like she told you that you were under a wandering spell." She picked up her spoon and sipped more of the stew. After her bowl was empty, she leaned back. "That door is gone. It opens for three days every three months in Everleaf and then it moves to a different location. And I know where it's going next."

"Can you show us?" he asked, still doubting her.

"We're ready to go," Elizabeth said. "We've just been waiting for you to wake up. Haline says she'll come with us to take me home."

He cut his eyes towards Haline, trying to discover a lie in what she'd told them. "Why are you helping us? Why haven't you turned us in?"

She smiled the same wicked expression she'd worn before she'd knocked him unconscious. "I can't let a defenseless child go to the weavers just because the princess doesn't have the balls to change her own damn laws."

With the morning sun to his back and a hammer in his hand, Grigory stood in front of the anvil. Usually, this was his favorite part: forming an untouched piece of steel into art. Today, however, his thoughts were elsewhere and he couldn't enjoy his work. Why did the boy take off? He knew Coal well enough to know why he took the girl. But where did Coal expect to go? How the hell did he expect to escape Princess Chalcedony and her horde?

Grigory had always suspected the boy was destined to be something more than the queenling's lackey. And when he'd told Grigory that he felt the soul in Chalcedony's sword, it was confirmed. No magic-less human should have been able to detect the sword's soul, especially if Grigory could not.

He was about to begin working when he felt a presence behind him. He turned. Once his eyes adjusted to the sun, he saw who it was. "Princess! I apologize. I didn't hear you." He placed his hammer on the anvil and bowed.

"I understand. You were occupied with other things." She stood across from him, wearing long black pants and a long-sleeved shirt.

"Have you found Coal and the girl?" He wiped the sweat from his brow and let hope seep into his voice.

"No." She walked casually around the outside of the forge until she was standing directly in front of him. "Do you know where they might be?"

"No, Princess."

"We don't talk much, but I know you and Coal are close. I also know you're a skilled fighter, not just a forger. The scars on your face …" She touched the scar underneath his missing eye. He grimaced as the flow of her power sent a sharp pain down his spine. "… are not from fire. Every soldier in my army fears and respects you. From what I remember, my mother always spoke well of you. But if I find out you know anything about where Coal is …" She paused, leaning in closer. "Or if I discover you were involved in any way, your reputation will not be able to save you."

"Coal is precious to me, but you represent the land that I love. I am your servant just as I was for your mother."

She shrugged as if she didn't believe him, or she didn't care. "Did you know he took my sword?"

"No, I didn't. That part of the story hadn't reached me."

Her mood had changed. The air shifted. Her hardness was replaced by an easy familiarity, but he didn't let himself relax.

"How long will it take to make me another?" she asked.

"You don't plan to have it back before your coronation?" He couldn't fathom Coal being gone much longer. He was barely older than a child. "It shouldn't take long to make another. There was a second sword almost as good."

"Almost as good? So I will have the second best?" she asked as if she already knew the answer.

"Finding something better would take more time, and I don't think you'd have it before your coronation."

"I already have one. I just need you to make sure I can use it." She pulled a wrapped sword from the sheath on her back and set it on the anvil next to the cooled metal. Grigory approached and slowly peeled back the leather wrapping.

"That's your mother's sword." He stepped back. "It's already been bonded."

"I know," she replied." Do you think I can use it?"

"Once a sword has been bonded, no one else can use it."

"I want this one," Princess Chalcedony said. "Fix it for me."

"There is nothing to fix."

"It doesn't matter. I want to take this one." She sounded as though she was asking for something simple and mundane, instead of something that had tried to kill her.

"Princess Chalcedony, this sword has already tried to kill you once. If you hadn't been a direct descendant of the queen, you would have died."

"When I touched it, it spoke to me. For a brief moment, it had accepted me. I loved my mother, but she has been gone for five years. Shouldn't it accept me now?"

"There is no way I can take away the bonding. But you're right. The binding magic could have naturally degraded to the point where it would accept a blood descendant."

She smiled and met his eyes. She'd made her decision before she'd approached him.

Before he could stop her, she reached for the unwrapped sword with her bare hands, lifted it, and looked squarely at Grigory. "I feel it. It's accepted me." Then, her knees buckled, and she fell onto the ash-covered ground.

Chalcedony slowly became aware of Madoc and Grigory arguing. From the warmth of the blanket wrapped around her, she knew she was in her own bed instead of lying in the dirt at Grigory's forge. Passing out had been embarrassing, but she'd done what she'd intended. Mayhem wanted to be wielded. She'd felt that when she'd touched it. She just needed to work around its binding. With a little practice, she knew she could do it. She sat up and yawned, amazed at how rested she felt.

"Are you okay, Princess?" Grigory asked.

"I'm fine. How long have I been asleep?"

"You were not asleep. You were unconscious." Madoc spoke as if he was accusing her of trying to commit suicide.

"But your breathing was steady, unlike last time," Grigory said. "You were only out for a few hours. When you were younger, you were out for two days."

"How could you have been so irresponsible to have let her use that weapon?" Madoc asked.

"Where is the sword?" Chalcedony didn't have the patience to listen to Madoc argue. She'd wasted too much time already.

"What do you mean where is the sword? You couldn't even touch it without passing out," Madoc said.

"I didn't die. That's a good sign." She stepped out of the bed, feeling rested and invigorated. It was time to start the hunt and bring Coal back. "Bring me the sword, Grigory. Madoc, tell the guards to prepare the dragons. We're leaving in twenty minutes."

Coal finished eating and stepped into the dwarf's living area. It was not much different from the room he'd woken in. An intricate web of tree and plant roots crisscrossed the ceiling and walls. Instead of dirt, wooden planks lined the floor. The planks squeaked as he walked on them.

Directly across from him, Elizabeth and Haline were stabbing a hay-filled dummy with a dagger.

"What's going on?" he asked.

"Haline is teaching me how to fight." Elizabeth jabbed at the figure twice as fast.

"You gave her a knife?"

"So?" Haline asked.

"She's too young."

"No, I'm not." Elizabeth stabbed the fake torso below its neck.

"There is no such thing as too young to use a knife," Haline said. "How are you feeling?"

Coal rubbed the back of his neck. "Much better. Maybe you were right about the wandering spell."

"I know I was right. We're leaving."

"How are we going to get past Chaley's soldiers? By now, they'll have noticed we're gone."

"Let me worry about that." She walked into the room he'd come from and returned with Mischief and a pair of black leather gloves.

"Something isn't right, Madoc." They had been flying over the forest for hours. There were on the ground now, letting the dragons rest. "There is no word from the prophets or truthsayers?"

"No, they haven't seen anything."

"Do you think it's possible Coal and Lizzy were able to travel to the human realm?"

"Impossible. The door closed days ago."

We're at a disadvantage. We need to recover it.

When she and Coal had played hide-and-seek as kids, she'd always beaten him. Always. Where was he now? You're not above me, she thought, staring at the grazing dragons. You're not in front of me.

"Madoc." Chalcedony stood and wiped the grass from her pants.

"Yes," he answered.

"Are there any gnomes or dwarves in these woods?"

"No, the forests were cleared centuries ago."

"Bring me Ambassador Eli. I need to ask him some questions."

CHAPTER ELEVEN

Coal had always had a fascination with caves and secret passageways, so he'd been excited when he'd first stepped into the dimly lit underground tunnel, but his eagerness had dissipated a few miles ago. The deeper they traveled along the tunnel, the hotter it became. It felt as if he'd been walking for days instead of a few hours.

Haline kept at least ten paces in front of Coal and Elizabeth. She looked as if she'd just begun the trek. Neither the heat nor the thin, dry air affected her.

"Can we stop, please?" Coal asked. Elizabeth lay limply on his back. He'd wanted to ask Haline to stop a mile back, but he didn't want the dwarf calling him weak. Haline could call him any name she liked as long as they stopped.

"No. Give me Elizabeth," Haline said. "We don't have far to go. You can rest later."

"You can't carry her," he said, mostly out of guilt. He was bigger and taller than Haline. He should have been strong enough to carry Elizabeth. "She's too heavy for you."

"Boy, if I can carry you from the forest to my home. I can carry this child for a few more miles."

Feeling guilty, he bent down and let Haline put Elizabeth on her back.

"It's hot." Elizabeth murmured while her cheek lay against Haline. Sweat prickled her forehead.

"It'll cool down in a minute." Haline quickened her pace.

Coal stretched the tight muscles of his back and neck before he followed. Heat permeated the tunnel, but without Elizabeth on his back it was easier to breathe.

"Why aren't you hot?" Even with Elizabeth straddled to her back, Haline gave no sign of fatigue.

"I'm a dwarf." She shuffled quickly along the tunnel. "I was raised to endure the heat of the forges. This is nothing."

Of course, the heat didn't affect her. Grigory was the same way. The swordsmith would be at the forge for hours, sometimes days, making a sword. *How could I have been a swordsmith if I couldn't even work the forge for more than a few hours?* He hadn't wanted to admit it, but what Madoc and Chalcedony had said was true: Grigory had only offered him the apprenticeship out of pity.

"Stop," Haline said, interrupting Coal's pity party.

"Ah!" screamed a blur that appeared in front of them. It took a second for Coal to register it. The thing had risen out of the ground.

"I scared ya." It laughed hysterically. "I scared ya. I scared ya."

He—or at least Coal thought it was he—wagged his green gnarly finger at them and danced in a circle. Coal had thought the creature was nude, but when he looked closer, he saw that its green skin was covered with patches of leaves, which wrapped around its body. He smelled of fresh earth after a heavy spring shower. It was a walking and talking mix between a plant and a tree.

"You didn't scare me." Haline knocked his stick-like hand away. He towered over Haline and Elizabeth, but only stood a head taller than Coal. "I knew you were there. You do this every time I come through."

He stopped laughing long enough to say, "Well, I scared your customers."

Coal exchanged a confused look with Elizabeth. Both of them had been surprised by the creature, but before any fear registered, the creature had already started snickering and dancing.

Abruptly, it stopped and narrowed its bright green eyes towards Haline. "What are you doing here anyway?" He focused his eerily intense eyes on Coal and Elizabeth. "Who is this? Your door closed days ago. You should not have any customers."

He paused for a long moment. "These are human children," he spat. The air in the tunnel became stifling with the smell of manure and rot. "Are these the children the queenling is looking for?"

"Calm down," Haline said.

"Calm down, calm down." The creature's voice became deeper. It echoed through the tunnels, shaking the floor and the walls.

"This is my cave. My cavern. I will not calm down." The parts of his skin not covered with leaves changed from green to black.

"You are supposed to transport humans from the queenling's door, not steal her playthings. Turn around and take them back!" He faced Coal and Elizabeth. Coal pushed Elizabeth behind him and took out his sword. Before the creature could get much closer, Haline pushed him.

"No, I will not take them back."

He stopped and directed his anger at Haline.

"Calm down now, Cesaro!" Haline stomped her feet, unsettling a cloud of dirt. "Go get Geric."

Cesaro lifted his knotted hand. Before Cesaro could hit Haline, Coal swung his sword towards the beast. The sound of metal against Cesaro's wooden skin vibrated through the cave. Coal stepped back, expecting some sort of damage, but Cesaro showed no sign that he had even been hit. Coal might as well have attacked the cave for the amount of damage he had done.

A wicked, deadly smile crossed his face. Coal tried to strike again, but the creature grabbed his sword hand and lifted him from the ground.

The pain in Coal's wrist was immeasurable. Rage filled the sword because it could not fight. Hands immobile, Coal kicked at Cesaro, but Cesaro ignored the thrusts.

Cesaro laughed. Unlike the joyful noise from earlier, it was deep, wicked, and made Coal's stomach twist with fear. Despite his dread, he glared into the creature's eyes. If he was going to die, he wanted to die fighting.

"Little human," Cesaro hissed. "This is my cave. Your people tried to kill my kind years ago, but I survived." He grabbed Coal's throat. Coal dropped his sword and clawed at the hand around his neck. "I was here before your kind, and I will be here after you are gone."

"Cesaro, you crazy bastard. Put the boy down!" Haline shouted.

Coal struggled to see past the light show playing havoc with his vision. He tried to tell Haline and Elizabeth to run, but he couldn't form the words.

"Put him down!" Haline screamed, repeatedly shoving the creature.

Through his blurry vision, Coal saw confusion and hesitation on the creature's face.

"ARRRRRR!" Cesaro screamed before he dropped Coal. "Stupid human," Cesaro said as Coal writhed on the ground.

Coal knew he was rolling in dirt and scratching his back on the jagged rocks, but the small stabs of pain were secondary to his need to breathe.

As his breathing evened out, Coal saw Cesaro staring down at Haline with fire in his eyes. She stared up at the creature with an unwavering gaze. Cesaro was no match for her because the creature's breathing slowed. Cesaro's skin changed from brown to green, and the fresh scent of earth replaced the stench of fertilizer once again.

"I like you, Haline," he said. "But I'm still not letting you pass."

"Go get the boss. If he tells me I have to turn back, then I will."

"I'll get him, dwarf, but if the queenling invades my cavern …"

"If you keep wasting time, she'll find us without a problem. It's much harder to catch a moving target."

He locked eyes with Coal for a moment before he disappeared into the ground.

Coal glanced back to check on Elizabeth. He'd expected to see her crouched in the corner, but she was only a few feet away with her dagger held tightly in her hand.

Crouched on all fours, Coal grabbed his livid sword.

You shouldn't have dropped me.

Well, he thought back at it, *a lot of good you did. We couldn't even leave a mark on him.*

Haline hung her head and sighed before she faced Coal and Elizabeth. "What are you looking so nervous for?"

"What was that?" Elizabeth asked. Her eyes were wide and wary as if waiting for Cesaro to materialize in front of them again.

Haline's expression softened. "Cesaro is a sweetheart. He wouldn't hurt a fly. He was just joking."

Elizabeth looked to Coal, waiting for confirmation, but he didn't know Cesaro. The creature's death-like grip on Coal's throat hadn't felt like a joke, but Coal grinned towards Elizabeth and said, trying to sound as if he was not in pain, "It didn't hurt me." *Much.*

Elizabeth put away her knife and stood next to Coal. She'd been favoring Haline since they'd started the journey. Coal wondered what had made the girl come near him this time. Did she suspect that Haline had been lying about Cesaro not being able to hurt a fly; or was she scared of a dwarf that stared down a monster without flinching?

"What was that?" Coal asked.

Haline's face hardened, and her eyes showed less sympathy.

"Cesaro is a spriggin. They guard caves and burrows. They've been used by dwarves for centuries to guard secret entrances."

Coal remembered briefly reading about spriggins in books. From what he'd read, the creatures were a distant relative of trees, like Legacy. "Aren't they supposed to be friendly?"

"Don't believe everything you read in a book. Spriggins were never friendly. They weren't exactly fearsome either."

"But this is a tunnel, not a cave," Coal said.

Haline cocked an eyebrow. "Really?"

Coal took a few steps forward. He was no longer in the tunnel, but a cavern.

A rippling blue-black lake lay in the middle of the 200-foot-wide cavern. Stone archways preceded extravagant, withering gray marble structures. Green vines and flowers draped around the immense stone columns and clambered inside the deserted buildings. The plants seemed to be the cavern's only inhabitants. Some of the buildings were so shrouded that they appeared to be carved from moss and dirt instead of stone.

"Where are all the people?" Elizabeth asked in wonder.

"There is no one here. It used to be a great dwarven city, but they ran out of gold, silver, and jewels, so the entire clan packed up everything and left," Haline said, while she slid her hand along the side of a building, her fingers leaving small indentations in the moss. "All great cities eventually die."

Elizabeth's wonder disappeared. She moved closer to Coal, as if she believed the fate of the abandoned city was contagious.

"Take a seat." Haline sat next to the lake. "This is the rest you were so anxious for."

Elizabeth sat cross-legged on the ground, pulled out her knife, and carved into the dirt. He followed them onto the ground. Weariness seeped into his bones as the adrenaline from the fight wore off.

Coal peered into the lake expecting to see fish, but, like the rest of the underground city, it was lifeless.

"Why did he say that we were customers?" Coal asked. "I don't have any money." He needed to know what was going on. Haline had said she'd take them to the door. She had never mentioned spriggins, underground caverns, or having a boss.

"I searched your pockets, boy. I know you don't."

"What was Cesaro talking about? Why can't we leave before he comes back?"

"My customers are fey and human. I lead them from Chalcedony's door to other parts of the fey realm."

Coal narrowed his eyes. "Isn't that illegal?"

"Yes, that's why it's called smuggling."

"Why do we have to wait for your boss? Cesaro is crazy. Can't we go without him?" Elizabeth asked.

Haline pointed towards the buildings. "You see the archways?"

Coal and Elizabeth nodded.

"There are ten of them. I have no idea how to get to Queen Isis's door from here. I'm new to this job. My role is to take the client safely through Chalcedony's forest, around the queenling's traps, and deliver them here. Someone else escorts them the rest of the way."

"The passageways were built to confuse outsiders that were not supposed to be here. Outsiders like you," said a deep male voice from behind.

Coal and Elizabeth jumped to their feet. Cesaro had returned. Standing next to him was a dark-haired, olive-skinned dwarf with hazel eyes. Haline snickered and slowly stood.

"Hello, Geric," she called.

Elizabeth promptly took her place behind Coal's leg. "Who is that?" she asked, whispering low enough for only Haline and Coal to hear.

"Geric's the boss," Haline said. "Both of you stay silent, and let me do the talking."

Geric walked to Haline and frowned. "Why did you bring them here?"

"I thought they were paying customers I'd missed somehow. Once I learned who they were, I couldn't leave them. The boy was cursed, and the girl was scared. They had no idea the door had moved."

"Why is that your problem? They are nothing to you or us."

"What's done is done." Haline met his gaze. It was the same stare she'd used on Cesaro.

Geric broke the silence. "I knew you would be trouble. You're right. We can't undo what has been done."

"But," Cesaro said, "helping them will get us—"

"Does Haline look like she's going to take them back?" Geric asked.

Cesaro rolled his eyes and glared at Coal. "No." His jaw twitched.

"I don't think so either. Arguing is only wasting time. If we act quickly, we may be able to salvage our business." Geric faced Haline. "What do you need me to do?"

"We need to get them to Queen Isis's door," Haline said.

"That should be easy enough." Geric motioned to Cesaro. "Find out where the princess is in her search for her lost toys."

Cesaro scowled, but mumbled, "Yes, sir," before he disappeared.

"Thanks, Geric," Haline said.

He closed the distance between the two of them. An uncomfortable silence filled the cavern. Both Geric and Haline stood still, waiting for the other to flinch. Coal wondered if there was about to be a fight, but Geric spoke. "As if I ever had a choice." Then he leaned in and placed his lips on hers. Haline stood still for a moment, but then she smiled and returned the kiss.

"Ewe, gross," Elizabeth said.

Coal looked around, wondering if he had missed something. After they separated, Haline smiled. "No, you never had a choice."

Geric left them alone in the cavern while he went to get supplies and their transport. Elizabeth was sleeping with her head resting on Coal's cloak. Coal, unable to sleep, watched Haline as she sharpened her dagger on a rock.

"Is smuggling people through Princess Chalcedony's door dangerous?" Coal asked.

Haline shrugged as she stroked the metal edge against the rock. "Yes. If I get caught, I'll probably be sent to the weavers. But Princess Chalcedony's mother was worse. She'd kill anyone—human or fey—that she found in her forest."

"You lied to him. You didn't think we were paying customers. The door was already closed."

She grinned. "Yeah. He knows I was lying. Relationships are built on lies."

"Do you really believe that?"

Chalcedony had never told him about the door moving or the wandering spell. She'd also lied about him having enough magic to travel through the portal. Elizabeth had more magic than him, and she was supposed to be magic null. Had he been naive to trust Chalcedony for so long?

Haline placed her sharpened dagger in its hilt. "This isn't about me and Geric. This is about you. Fey tell themselves lies every day. Have you ever paid attention to the tailor and his young wife? She's too young for him, but she has nimble fingers and knows what the younger generation wants. She uses him for money and security. He uses her to increase his profits. He turns his back when she disappears for a couple of hours every other week. But I've seen them together. They love each other. They selfishly tell lies so that they can be happy together. The entire realm knows how much you love the princess, but you still chose to betray her. Does that mean you love her any less?"

"But—"

"But what?" Geric asked. The raven-haired dwarf stood in one of the grand archways next to a very large spider. No, it wasn't a spider. It was a spidren. It stood as tall as one of Chalcedony's royal horses, and it was three times as wide. Coal had heard horror stories about them. He'd always thought—hoped—they were a myth. From the stories, spidrens had mandibles that opened and stretched in four directions to swallow their victims whole.

As if Elizabeth sensed Coal's fear, she chose that moment to wake. Her eyes settled on the spidren. She shrieked, crawled up Coal as if she were a spider herself, and buried her head in his shoulders.

"Don't be scared," Geric said gently. He and the spidren left the archway and walked further into the cavern. "This is Astra. She can deliver you to Queen Isis's door faster than a horse or a flying dragon."

"I don't bite. I promise," the spidren said with a scratchy hiss. Astra's voice made Elizabeth's trembling increase tenfold.

"Do you still want to go home?" Haline asked.

After a long pause, Elizabeth lifted her head. "I'm scared of spiders." Tears pooled in her eyes and fell onto the ground.

"I am not a spider," Astra hissed.

Spooked by Astra's voice, Elizabeth tried to bury her head in Coal's shoulder again.

"Astra is not a mindless spider," Haline said. "She is a spidren. She is smarter and nicer than you and I. Do you understand?"

Elizabeth dared a quick look at Astra before she jerked her head back towards Coal.

Haline silently pleaded with Coal to say something. She'd stared down a seven-foot-tall angry spriggin and forced her boss to do something he didn't want to, but convincing a child to overcome her fear of spiders was a power that Haline didn't have.

Coal didn't want to have anything to do with the giant spider either, but he swallowed his fear. "Lizzy, I know you're scared of …" He hesitated as he tried to remember the spidren's name. "… Astra, but if you want to get home, you have to act like a soldier. Soldiers don't cry, remember? A soldier wouldn't let fear keep her from getting home."

After a long moment, she said, "Okay. I'll try not to be scared."

With Elizabeth still in his arms, he walked towards Astra and then placed the little girl on the ground. He steeled himself before he faced the spidren. "We're ready to go."

"Just think of me as a giant horse." Astra smiled, showing four large, hairy, contracting pincers. Her breath smelled of rotten meat. A wisp of saliva dripped down her stubbly chin and fell onto the ground. "I am the fastest there is down here."

Coal swallowed his fear. "Okay, I'll go first." He fought the urge to flinch as he placed his hands on the side of Astra's bulbous body. The tiny hairs covering her back stuck to him uncomfortably as he climbed on.

"You need to place your feet right here." Geric pointed to where Astra's two front legs joined her abdomen. "It'll give you support and stop you from falling. Lizzy, you'll need to hold on to Coal."

Coal placed his feet between the joints. "What am I supposed to hold on to?" he asked, after he noticed there were no reins.

"If she keeps a steady pace, you won't need any reins. Your legs should be all you need," Geric said.

"Come on, Lizzy, let's go," Coal said, once he felt as if he wouldn't fall from Astra's back. Astra kneeled, and Geric placed Elizabeth behind Coal. Elizabeth's eyes were closed, but she didn't cry as she held on to his chest.

"Help me up, Geric," Haline said.

"No." Geric faced Haline. "This isn't your route."

Haline narrowed her eyes. "It won't hurt if I know the way."

"Astra and I will take them the rest of the way." Geric softened his voice. "I don't think we can trust you with another route yet. It's for everyone's protection. We've already bypassed enough rules."

"I promise to take good care of them, Haline," Astra hissed as gently as her scratchy voice would allow.

"But, Geric—"

"I'll protect them with my life," Geric said. "You know the rules. If you get caught knowing the entire route, we're all out of business."

"Fine. Just make sure they make it safely." Haline patted the spidren on the side. "Lizzy, you're the soldier, watch over Coal. Don't let anything happen to him. And you …" She scowled, looking towards Coal. "Stay alert. Don't make Lizzy do all the work."

"This is it." Ambassador Eli held a withered map in his hands. "Centuries ago, this was used as a secret entrance." He pointed to the only lifeless tree in the forest. The bark was completely stripped away, exposing the white and gray surface underneath. An eagle sat on her nest at the top, watching Chalcedony and the rest of her crew with a sharp, wary eye.

"I don't see a door. How do we get in?" Chalcedony asked.

The dwarf bit his lip before he circled the large tree. He looked up and down as he went. Once he'd completed his inspection, he touched the tree. The eagle leaned over her nest and squawked. The dwarf flinched and hurried back to Chalcedony.

"I suppose the map doesn't say how to get in?" Chalcedony asked.

"No, Princess." Ambassador Eli stared nervously at the eagle.

"Of course, it wouldn't."

The eagle looked at Chalcedony through narrowed, suspicious eyes as she approached its home. She stared back at it, daring the mighty bird to attack her. It must have understood the threat because the eagle broke her gaze and began pruning her wings.

There was no obvious door here, so it had to be hidden by magic. Chalcedony placed her hands on the decrepit tree and concentrated. It wasn't dead. It was as old as the forest, but the roots still fed on the water from the soil and the branches still grabbed at sunlight for nourishment. Finally, the magic within the tree snagged on her own. She pushed it back through her fingertips and an eight-foot-high opening appeared on the side of the tree.

Not knowing what to expect, Chalcedony carefully leaned over. The tree was hollow with a staircase descending into the ground. "This is it."

"Princess, I should go before you." Avonnah placed a hand on her shoulder. Chalcedony stopped and gave the hand a long, hard glare.

"Get your hand off me." Madoc had given both Djamel and Avonnah a verbal thrashing on their inability to protect her. But their job had never been to protect her. Their job was to fight alongside her. Chalcedony should have seen the kick coming. She should have protected herself.

Avonnah removed her hand and shrunk away. "I apologize, Princess."

"Follow me," Chalcedony commanded.

The stairs took them to an underground home with four wooden columns holding up the ceiling. Candles aligned the walls. There was no one there, but she knew someone lived there. A female, Chalcedony sensed. Her energy touched everything. And mixed with it: the unmistakable smell of Coal and Elizabeth. The child had a scent she could only describe as human and young.

Finally, they were getting somewhere. "Search this place. There should be a tunnel."

"In here," Ambassador Eli said.

She followed his voice to a dining room filled with pots, pans, and a dwarven table with four chairs. Ambassador Eli stared at a dirt wall. "It should be here."

Just as she'd done with the tree, she rubbed her hands along the wall, feeling for its magic. Small flakes of dirt fell onto the ground as she traced her hands against the barrier. But there was nothing except for a dirt wall.

"Are you sure it's here?" she asked.

He looked nervously at the map. "Yes."

"How do you open?" she asked, remembering the hidden entrance on the tree.

"I don't know," Ambassador Eli said.

"I'm not talking to you."

He cocked an eyebrow. "Oh."

"How do you open?"

Once more, she placed her hands on the wall, feeling for anything unusual. She grinned when her finger came against a small circular bulge. She pushed it, and a section of the wall moved upwards. Her smile disappeared when she saw an entrance barely big enough for a dwarf.

CHAPTER TWELVE

Chalcedony moved through the tunnel on her hands and knees, making a mental note to start carrying gloves as the grit and dirt cut into her hands. After half a mile of crawling, the tunnel's ceiling was higher and they were able to stand. She stretched her achy back and looked around.

"They couldn't have passed through here more than a few hours ago, Princess." Avonnah inspected the half-burned candles along the wall.

"Good. If we run we'll catch up to them sooner." Chalcedony sprinted away, not waiting for a response. They knew to follow.

An hour later, they were still running. Chalcedony's legs throbbed, but each time she thought of stopping she made herself move faster. She was close to catching them. She had to be. The thought of losing them because she wasn't fast enough was all the fuel she needed to move quicker.

Running into a wall as she turned the next bend jostled her out of her thoughts. Gasping from exhaustion and disbelief, she realized the ceiling had collapsed, completely blocking the rest of the tunnel. She placed her hand onto the barrier, hoping to push it away. A few clumps of dirt and stone fell, but more took its place. The rest of her soldiers turned the corner and stopped before they collided with the wall.

"Dig." She faced the wall and snatched clumps of dirt and rock from the obstruction.

"Princess." Ambassador Eli gasped for breath. "This could take hours or days to excavate."

Chalcedony dropped the clump of dirt she had in her hand. "Are you sure?"

"Yes. It's a common defense mechanism. If they think they are being followed, they cave-in the tunnels."

"Why didn't you say anything before?" Avonnah asked, sweat dripping down her tired face.

The dwarf cowered. Then he must've remembered who he was because he stuck out his chest and raised his chin. "I am an ambassador, not a soldier. Nor do I work in the mines. Dwarves have been doing this for centuries. It's impossible to anticipate everything."

Chalcedony looked at the candles on the wall. All of the candles were still only halfway melted.

She touched one of the candles, expecting to get burned, but it was cool to the touch. It radiated heat, but it didn't burn her hand. When she tilted it, the wax didn't drip onto the ground.

"What's wrong with this candle?" Chalcedony asked, handing it to Ambassador Eli. He inspected the candle, turning it over as Chalcedony had done.

"It's not like any candle I have ever seen," he said.

"It looks like a candle, but it doesn't use wax," Chalcedony pointed out.

"But there's wax dripping down the side." Avonnah's voice was full of curiosity.

"It's only decorative," Ambassador Eli said, confirming what Chalcedony had guessed.

"We were using the candle as an indicator of how much time they had on us. They could be one day ahead or an hour." Avonnah threw up her hands in frustration.

"Ambassador, why didn't you know about this?" Chalcedony tried not to let disappointment show in her voice.

"I've never seen a candle like this. It's old magic, like the door hidden in the tree."

Dammit! Dammit! Dammit! She threw the candle onto the ground and then kicked it away. They'd come all this way for nothing. Why was tracking down two human children turning out to be so hard? She bit her lip, aware that her soldiers and Ambassador Eli were waiting for her to tell them what to do. She stifled a sigh of frustration and exhaustion. She should have been able to sense the magic in the candles. When this was over, she was going to study old magic; specifically, old dwarven magic.

"We have to go back. The ambassador is right. It could take hours to dig through this. If Coal is still trying to get Lizzy home, then he can only be headed to one place."

Madoc eyed the dozens of green and tan tents as he rode through Chalcedony's camp. What had started as a small search party for two humans had blossomed into preparation for full-out war. She'd requested most of her soldiers and taken the dragon riders away from their patrols.

The scent of sweat, horse manure, dragon dung, and roasted pig permeated the air. Some of the soldiers were practicing drills, but most were sitting outside of their tents laughing and eating.

Madoc nodded as he passed the two personal guards, Mahala and Jin, which he'd assigned to Chalcedony. Mahala's pale skin refused to tan even in the sun. She was thin with an unhealthy yellow tinge to her skin, but he knew she was not only strong, but quick, just like her partner. Jin may have been one of the oldest soldiers on active duty, but he was still stronger than most of the soldiers, and he had an eye for strategy. He couldn't have picked two better soldiers to look over Chalcedony.

She'd always refused personal guards. Her shadows were good enough, she'd said. Djamel and Avonnah were good shadows, but they were meant to track rogue fey in the human realm and that was best with soldiers that were trained as she was trained. Unfortunately, it also made them just as young and inexperienced as her.

This campaign of hers had given him an excuse to force Chalcedony to take personal guards, experienced fighters that could hold their own in either realm.

In the tent, Chalcedony stood over a table studying maps of dwarven tunnel routes.

She frowned. "Hello, Madoc. What brings you out in the field?" Her eyes were red and weary. He'd only seen her this tired after her mom had died, and she'd been unable to sleep for a week.

"You mean, why am I here, instead of at Legacy taking care of your duties?"

"I've been in the human realm longer than this with no complaints. Why are you complaining now?"

"This is different. You and your shadows are the only ones with the skills and the authority who can patrol our region of the human realm, but your presence here is unnecessary. You should leave this search to one of your senior soldiers and return to Legacy."

"Why would I want to do that?"

"Because you've dispatched most of your army to search for two human children as if you were going to war."

She leaned forward, placed her hands on the table, and glared at him. "You told me if I didn't punish Lizzy I would look weak in front of the realm. At your request, I made plans to imprison a child. But my best friend appointed himself her protector and they escaped. You were wrong about disciplining the child. I should have let it go. Now a small thing has become a huge thing. I will not let Coal get away with betraying me." She leaned back and put her hands behind her head. "No, I'll take care of this myself."

He'd expected to find her demoralized and ready to return home, but she was still confident despite her failures.

"How do you think it looks when you deploy an army to look for two human children?" When she didn't speak, he answered his own question. "It looks foolish."

"It looks like I will do whatever it takes to get back what's mine," she answered coldly. Her eyes were steady and determined. So she wasn't going to give up her search—*good. But I still need to play my part.*

"Have you thought about what you're going to do when you find them?" Madoc asked.

"They'll be punished."

"How?" he asked.

She rolled her eyes and smirked.

"I won't complain anymore about the resources you're using, but be prepared to finish what you've started," Madoc said. "Once you find them, you cannot show them mercy, nor redemption, nor pity."

She glared at him. "I've done that before."

"You have never punished someone you have loved. But every queen has been betrayed by a loved one. You are not the first. You will not be the last. Prepare yourself for what you'll have to do once you find them."

She stared down at the table, silent.

"I'm leaving. Think hard about their punishment. The resources you are using are great, so their punishment will have to be the same. If you are going to use everything you have, don't hesitate to strike, and above all, don't lose."

She looked up sternly. "I never lose."

That's my girl, he thought as he left.

"This is fun," Elizabeth said after they had been traveling for a while. When they had begun, Elizabeth had been a huddled, shivering mess, holding onto Coal with a death grip. After nothing happened, Elizabeth relaxed. Riding Astra wasn't much different than riding a horse. Except Astra was faster, had a smoother ride, and she spoke.

"When we get to my house you can meet my dad." Elizabeth interrupted Coal's thoughts. "He is always super busy, but sometimes we play video games together or watch kung fu movies."

Coal had no idea what she meant by video games or kung fu. "I'm just going to take you home. Then, I'm coming back."

"Is that wise?" Geric sat cross-legged on the spidren. He was both strong and experienced enough to stay on without having to use his legs to keep him upright. "If you return, the princess will send you to the weavers. What about your parents?"

"I was homeless when Chalcedony found me."

"Maybe you can live with me," Elizabeth said, just as Astra stopped abruptly.

"What's going on?" Geric asked. "Why are we stopping?"

"I feel something." Astra lowered her head.

"Like what?" Coal asked.

Astra moved sideways and placed one her front legs on the side of the tunnel. "The wall is vibrating."

Coal, Lizzy, and Geric put their hands on the wall. There was a steady, strong pulse, like a heartbeat emanating through it.

"What's that?" Elizabeth asked, her nervous voice breaking the silence.

"Nothing." Geric removed his hand from the wall. "It's probably some farmers tilling their land. Keep moving, Astra."

She moved away from the wall and quickened her pace. Her body stiffened in a way that hadn't been there before. A flake of dirt fell from above and landed in Elizabeth's hair. As Coal watched, more flakes fell. The wizard lights along the wall flickered.

"It's snowing dirt." Elizabeth caught some of the specks in her hand. Giant clumps of rock and clay dropped next to them.

"It's a cave-in," Geric cried. "Run!"

"Hold on." Astra moved faster, trying to outrun the falling earth and rocks. A large boulder fell in front of her. She dodged it, but the quick change of direction sent Geric, Coal, and Elizabeth onto the ground. Before Coal thought to move, Geric leaped onto Astra's nearest leg and climbed back onto the spidren.

"Get up!" Geric screamed. "Hand me the girl!"

Spurred into action, Coal picked up Elizabeth and handed her to Geric. He was about to follow when the entire ceiling collapsed, covering everything in a suffocating darkness. Instinctively, Coal used his arms to cover his head. Before he knew it, he was crouched in a ball, restricted on all sides by chunks of dirt and rock.

Panicking, he tried to stand, hoping if he stood straight he'd be above the cave-in. But there was so much earth and rock that he didn't know which way was up. Terrified, he dug through the rubble. His lungs burned from lack of air while he fought his way to the top.

Someone grabbed his hand.

He was so relieved that he forgot to hold his breath. Dirt filled his mouth and he gagged on rocks and earth until he was mercifully pulled through the rubble and into the sunlight. On his hands and knees, he coughed up soil and rock, opening his dirt-covered eyes and expecting to see Geric and Elizabeth.

His blood turned to ice and dread replaced his elation.

"Hello, Coal," Djamel said, with a dark, humorless smile.

CHAPTER THIRTEEN

Djamel grabbed the front of Coal's shirt and lifted the boy onto his feet. "Don't think about fighting me. Before you could try anything, I'd have both of your hands cut off. As pleasurable as that would be for me, the princess would be disappointed if she wasn't allowed to dismember you herself."

"How did you find us?" Coal asked, his voice raspy and his throat sore from coughing.

"You could only be headed to one place." Chalcedony approached from behind Djamel. She beamed with triumph as if she'd just won another running race. If he'd been successful at getting Elizabeth home, he would have gladly faced her and accepted his punishment. Now, he couldn't meet her eyes. He turned away, feeling like a failure.

In all of the commotion, Coal had forgotten about everybody else. Astra had climbed out of the hole, and Elizabeth was clinging to her back. They were surrounded by twelve heavily armed soldiers pointing their swords nervously at the giant spider.

"Give up the girl!" Avonnah shouted to Astra.

"No," Astra hissed. She opened and closed her pincers as a white viscous liquid dripped from her mouth and onto the ground. The docile spidren had been replaced by the nightmare everyone had been taught to fear.

Chalcedony directed her attention from Astra and back towards Coal. "Djamel, take him to his tent. I'll take care of this."

"Yes, Princess," Djamel said.

Coal tried to follow Chalcedony towards Elizabeth and Astra, but Djamel pulled him by the shoulder in the opposite direction. "Your part in this game is over. There's nothing you can do for them."

Djamel dragged him passed endless rows of tents. Only a fraction of Chalcedony's soldiers were near the tunnel. Dozens more were still in the camp. When the soldiers saw Djamel pulling Coal through the tents, they stopped what they were doing and stared. Some smiled. All had the look of victory on their faces.

They never had a chance, Coal thought, as he took in the hundreds of tents and supplies Chalcedony had brought with her. How could he have competed against all of this?

Djamel stopped at a green tent and pushed Coal inside. "Sit." He motioned towards an old, dingy cot.

Coal did as ordered and faced Djamel. "I'm sorry about the sleeping powder."

"Sorry?" he repeated in an accusing tone that made Coal flinch. "That stunt got me demoted from number one to number two, and the princess took away my sword."

Coal chanced a quick glance at Djamel's sword. The hilt was different than the one he had delivered to the soldier a few days ago. The position of a shadow was a revered position, and shadow number one was as good as it got. "I didn't think it would get you in trouble."

"Did you think at all? How could you have possibly thought it was a good idea to run off with that girl?"

"Someone had to do something."

"You are nothing. You have no power. What could you have possibly done for her?"

"We got this far."

"With luck. Now your luck is over. Sit down. Don't say another word or I will knock your teeth out."

Coal bit his lip and stayed silent. Guilt sat in his stomach like a heavy stone. Djamel had been one of the few fey who had shown him any respect. He'd lost Chalcedony and Djamel's trust, and it had all been for nothing.

Before Chalcedony entered the tent, she ordered Mahala and Jin, the guards Madoc had assigned her, to stay outside. She expected a protest, but they nodded and stood on both sides of the entrance. Madoc couldn't fool her. They were there to report every move she made. She would have done the same thing if she were him. Being spied on or not, she needed to understand why Coal had betrayed her.

The urge to go back to her tent and change out of the dirty clothes she'd worn for the past two days had been intense. But she'd fought the vain impulse. She was going to meet a prisoner, not a date.

A suffocating anxiety had been crushing her over the past few days, but now breathing came easy again. Coal had put up a good chase, but she'd won. She'd found him. He lay before her on a cot while Djamel stood motionless across from him.

"You can leave," she told Djamel.

He nodded and walked out. She'd hesitated to assign him to guard Coal, thinking his anger might cause Djamel to hurt Coal. But she didn't trust anyone but Djamel to be alone with her prisoner. The elf was the best fighter she had and never questioned her orders.

Avonnah, on the other hand, always second-guessed Chalcedony and had a tendency to act first and apologize later. She was good in a fight, but Chalcedony didn't trust the soldier with delicate matters.

Chalcedony stood over Coal while he lay with his eyes closed. The tailored clothes he'd worn the night of the party were covered in dirt, mud, and blood. Grime filled his nails and his fingers were bleeding From what she saw, there was no serious damage. She should have been angry, but she'd won. He was back. Now what?

"You miss me?" Coal finally asked, with a sarcastic grin, eyes still closed.

"Why did you do it?" she asked, kicking the side of this cot.

He sat up and stared at her with bloodshot eyes. "I didn't have a choice."

"There is always a choice."

"The same applies to you. You're about to be queen. You have the power to forgive and forget, but you let Madoc condemn a child," he bellowed.

Chalcedony rolled her eyes. She had nothing to feel guilty about. He was the one who had betrayed her.

"I listen to Madoc because he has served my family for centuries. He is always right, just like he was right about you. I should have left you in the human realm.

"You should have trusted me," Chalcedony continued. "Yes, I was going to send Lizzy to the weavers, but she would have had everything she asked for while she was there. When the door was back in my forest, I was going to send her home."

Coal eyed her sharply. "Why didn't you tell me that?"

She sat next to him on the hard cot. "You didn't give me a chance."

"I thought—" Coal stuttered.

"You thought I would send a child to the weavers to be tortured and worked to death."

He paused, the answer clearly on his face.

"Do you think I'm evil?"

"I-I—" he stuttered. "Well, Madoc—"

"I'm going to be queen. I need to be respected and feared. But you know me. You should have trusted me not to hurt her."

He studied his hands while he thought of the right words. "The Chaley I know is different from Chalcedony-the-would-be-queen. I didn't know what to do." He paused. "I'm sorry. You're right. I should have trusted you. What happens next?"

"I wish I could say that we were headed back to Legacy, and Lizzy was going back to the human realm, but too much has happened."

"Take Lizzy home, Chaley. I'll take the punishment for both of us."

Madoc had told her not to show mercy, but she hadn't thought about Coal's punishment. Not even after Madoc had told her to. "I need time to think."

He nodded. "Why didn't you tell me the door to the human realm moves?"

She chose her words carefully. "No one is supposed to know it exists. I'm used to being secretive about it, so I didn't tell you. Madoc let us go because he thought I was going to leave you there."

"Why did you choose her over me?" The question made her feel weak. She should be above jealousy, but she had to know.

"I didn't choose her over you. We promised to take her home."

"But you were leaving me." Chalcedony concentrated on a stain on the tent's wall while she listened to his answer.

"As soon as she was back in the human realm, I was coming back."

She glanced at him through the corner of her eye. He was looking forward. They were both scared to face each other, to ask questions, and probably more frightened of the answers.

"You were returning even though you knew you'd be punished?" Chalcedony asked.

"Where else would I go? This is the only home I know." He grinned, all teeth and dimples. "And maybe I was hoping that eventually you'd forgive me."

"Did you?" She smiled despite herself. *Would I have forgiven him? Have I already forgiven him?*

"My turn now," he said. "Why was there a wandering spell on me?"

That was easy. "In case you wandered off or ran away. My mother put it on you the day you arrived."

"You didn't trust me enough to tell me?"

"It was a long time ago. I forgot. It obviously didn't work, if you made it this far."

"It worked." He looked away, eyes distant again.

"Then how come you're not sick?"

"Luck." He motioned towards the sword at her waist. "Why do you have your mother's sword?"

Chalcedony was more than a little curious to find out how he circumvented the wandering spell, but she didn't press it. There would be plenty of time to ask questions later. She'd have a better spell put on him later. "You took my sword. So you gave me an excuse to use my mother's."

"But isn't it still enchanted? Can't it kill you?" He sounded worried, almost like they were friends again.

"I passed out at first, but now it's getting used to me." She'd been practicing with it over the past few days. In each session, she'd increased the amount of time she'd held it. It still fought her, but she hadn't fainted again. Afterward, she'd had a headache for a few hours, but it was worth it. "Why did you take my sword anyway?"

"I thought we might need some protection in the forest and—" Coal hesitated.

"You're in love with it," Chalcedony finished for him. "The same way I'm in love with my mother's sword."

He laughed as he eyed Mischief strapped to her back. Her mother's sword was sheathed at her waist. It couldn't hurt to have two swords. Was it even possible to train with two sentient swords? Would one be jealous of the other?

"Yes, I'm in love with it," Coal said. "Your mother's sword is beautiful, but it doesn't compare to yours."

She shrugged. "Maybe. We'll argue about it after I decide on your punishment for leaving me and taking my sword. Right now, I have to make sure everything and everyone is packed and ready to go."

For the past few days, she'd been working on nothing but adrenaline. Now that the search was over, she was ready to sleep for a week. She stood and stretched, once again, noticing Coal's scratches. "I'll have someone bring you food and see to your wounds."

"One more question," he said as she was leaving. Chalcedony paused. "How are Astra, Lizzy, and Geric?"

Chalcedony rolled her eyes. "The spidren refused to give up Lizzy, and the girl refused to let go. So I let them stay together on the promise that the spidren wouldn't cause any trouble." She had been more than willing to leave them alone. The damn spidren freaked her and the soldiers out. Besides, Elizabeth couldn't stay attached to it forever. As soon as Elizabeth was free of it, Chalcedony had told Avonnah to grab her.

"What about—" Coal began, but Chalcedony left before he could ask her any more questions. She always liked to have the last word.

True to her word, Chalcedony had a bucket of soapy water and a towel sent to him so he could wash his face and hands. Then a healer came to wrap his wounds and gave him a pungent tea that helped sooth his aching body. Afterward, he sat on a clean cot devouring roasted pork garnished with carrots and apples. The sweetness of the fruit perfectly complemented the succulent, salty meat. It would have felt like home except for Djamel standing near the entrance, grasping the hilt of his sword with the corner of his lip turned up in a sneer.

Coal leaned back and licked his fingers. He should have been scared and nervous, but it was hard not to be optimistic about the future when he was eating so well.

Djamel gritted his teeth. "Princess Chalcedony has done nothing but protect you since you've been in this realm. She has done nothing but …" He lifted a corner of his lip in disgust. "… love you. But you ran away with that child without a word. And now you sit here eating her food and smiling shamelessly. Tell me, human, what type of person does that make you?"

His appetite suddenly gone, Coal sat back and took a long deep breath. "What else could I have done?" Coal asked. "Chalcedony had agreed to send Elizabeth to a torture camp. I had no other choice."

Just as Djamel opened his mouth to respond, something hit the top of the tent with a wet and sticky thud that made Coal's skin crawl.

"What's going on?" Coal asked, jumping to his feet.

"Shut up." Djamel unsheathed his sword.

Seconds later, a scream pierced the silence.

"Aren't you going to see what's happening?" Coal asked, with a mixture of fear and curiosity.

"You are more important than whatever's happening outside. I'm staying right here." Djamel's eyes were wary as he stared at the entrance of the tent with his weapon ready. But no one entered. Instead, the tent disappeared and the star-filled sky appeared above their heads.

No, it hadn't disappeared, Coal realized. A dragon had it in its claws while it flew away. The beast landed a few yards away, tearing and gnawing at the tent as if it was a chew toy.

"What's going on?" Djamel asked, his voice filled with dismay and shock.

A quarter of the tents in the camp were being destroyed as dragons tore them apart. The beasts that were not chewing on tents were wrestling with other dragons or clashing with soldiers. Coal peered through the darkness towards the dragon on their tent. Raw bloody meat and entrails covered the tent.

Just as the dragon snapped towards Coal, Djamel pulled him away.

"What the hell are you doing? We've got to find cover. Come with me," Djamel ordered, his grip digging into Coal's elbow. They had almost made it to the forest when Coal saw Haline stalking towards them holding a bucket.

"Haline!" Coal screamed, resisting Djamel's pull. The dwarf wore battle armor that made her bosom ten times larger than Coal had remembered. Carved on each breast was a golden snake chasing and devouring its own tale. Despite the ongoing chaos, both Coal and Djamel stopped to stare. "Eyes up here," Haline said. "It's meant to distract the enemy, not you, Coal."

Coal shook his head and averted his eyes. "What are you doing here?"

No longer enthralled with the enchanting breastplate, Djamel lifted his sword and moved between Coal and Haline. "Who are you? If you've come for the boy, you're wasting your time."

"Really?" Haline lifted her bucket and threw it at Djamel. Blood and innards covered Djamel from the waist down. Gory pieces of raw flesh stuck to his clothes before dropping to the ground. Djamel looked down at himself before he glared hatefully at Haline.

He swung his sword towards her, but Haline, the only person Coal knew that moved faster than Djamel, was already gone. A dragon, attracted by the carrion, charged Djamel before he could find Haline. He sliced the beast's two front legs and it fell in an awkward thud to the ground as it yelled and screeched in pain.

Before Djamel caught his breath, one of the biggest dragons Coal had ever seen appeared from above. It dug it's talons into Djamel's shoulder and lifted him into the air.

Taken by surprise, Djamel dropped his sword. Coal caught his leg, the extra weight preventing the dragon from carrying Djamel away.

"Stupid, boy. Let him go!" Haline shouted from below.

"No! Help me!" Coal pleaded.

"He's a damn soldier. Let him go."

Djamel yelled as the dragon's talons pierced deeper into his flesh. The dragon flapped its wings, trying to gain more height.

"Help me, Haline!" Coal pulled Djamel's leg. "He's a friend." Or at least he had been. They weren't friendly now, but Djamel didn't deserve to be eaten by an out-of-control dragon. "I'm not leaving until I know he's safe."

"Damn it." Haline picked up Djamel's sword, spun three times and then loosed it. It ripped through one of the dragon's wings. The injured dragon gave a bone-rattling shriek before it fell to the ground with Djamel.

Even as the dragon lay writhing in pain, it refused to release its prey. Coal pulled at Djamel's arms, but the dragon snapped its bloodstained teeth at Coal, opening a gash on the back of his hand.

"Damn stupid boy," Haline muttered. "Leave it alone. I'll take care of it." She approached the dragon, stopping near the middle of its head, out of reach of the beast's line of sight. Then she plunged her dagger into its forehead. The dragon seemed as if it was about to let out another angry howl, but no sound escaped. The dragon's eyes closed, its breathing stopped, and Djamel fell from its grip. Coal took his uninjured hand and helped Djamel stand.

"You okay?" Haline asked Djamel.

"Yes." He rubbed his injured shoulder.

Haline cocked an eyebrow. "Don't thank me yet." She pulled back her small fist and punched him in the groin.

Djamel doubled over in pain, and she hit him on the head with the butt of her dagger. The metal made a loud thump as it connected with Djamel's head and sent the soldier falling onto the ground.

"Why did you do that?" Coal asked, eyes wide and mouth wide open in dismay.

"Wasn't he guarding you?" Haline asked.

"Yes, but he was hurt." Coal leaned over and checked Djamel's breathing. Djamel lay unconscious, but he still breathed.

"Was he the type that would just let you walk away?" Haline asked, with her hands defiantly on her waist.

"No," Coal answered reluctantly. Djamel had already told Coal he'd rather die than let Coal escape again.

"I didn't think so." Haline tore a piece of the cloak attached to the back of her breastplate. "Let me see your hand."

"Why?" Coal asked, suddenly wary.

"You're bleeding, dumbass. Let me wrap it."

"Oh."

Fresh waves of pain shot through his hand and up his arm as she wrapped it.

When she had finished, Haline shoved his hand away. "We need to get everyone else."

"But we can't leave Djamel here. We have to at least hide him so he doesn't get hurt."

She cocked an eyebrow. "I'm not protecting him. You go ahead. Waste our time and put this whole rescue mission at risk while you try to save your enemy." She crossed her arms in front of her golden bosom. "I'll wait here."

He tried not to look at her large chest. "It'll go faster if you help."

"No. He's your friend, not mine." She tapped her foot.

Ignoring the pain in his hand, Coal pulled Djamel into to the forest and covered his body with leaves and dirt. He was sure the dragons would smell him, but he hoped the beasts wouldn't want to work that hard to sniff him out when there was easily available food at the camp.

He stood and wiped the dirt from his hands onto his pants. A strong sense of déjà vu suddenly flooded over him.

Djamel was going to really hate him now.

CHAPTER FOURTEEN

"Wear this. We need to find the others before the queenling can get her soldiers organized." Haline threw Djamel's bloody cloak at Coal.

Behind the safety of the trees, Coal put on the cloak and surveyed the camp. The once orderly site had turned into a horrific dream. A few soldiers, most still in their nightclothes, were wrestling the tents from the dragons. Some tents were on fire and a group of soldiers were trying to quench the blaze.

"Where are they?" Coal asked.

Haline shrugged. "I don't know where they are. I'm lucky I found you."

"What do you mean you don't know where they are? What if they're already dragon food?"

"If they're as guarded as you were, then they're okay," Haline said.

"Make sure you keep your head down. If we stay near the trees, we shouldn't be seen."

Coal nodded and followed Haline as she crept along the tree line.

What am I doing? Coal thought as he clambered over tree roots and fallen branches. A few minutes ago, he had been sitting in a tent, comfortable, warm, and safe. Why was he here now? Chalcedony had forgiven him. Hadn't she? No. She had said she needed time to think. But what if he was making things worse?

"Wait," he said to Haline. Maybe they could trust Chalcedony. When Haline didn't stop, he spoke louder. "Haline, wait. We don't have to do this …"

They both stopped when they saw Geric being chased by a dragon twice the dwarf's size. While they watched, the dragon jumped onto Geric's back and bit into the dwarf's shoulder.

"Distract the dragon, and I'll do the rest," Haline commanded.

"How?" Coal asked, but Haline had already started creeping towards the beast.

Gathering his courage, Coal moved towards the back of the dragon.

Geric had managed to roll over onto his back, and now the dragon had Geric's forearm in its mouth.

Before he lost his nerve, Coal jumped onto the dragon's back. He landed between its wings and wrapped his arms around its thick neck. In protest, the dragon stood on its hind legs, lifting Coal eight feet in the air.

The beast clawed at Coal's hands, aggravating the cut he'd already received. Despite the searing pain, Coal refused to let go. The dragon had released Geric and now he stared at Coal with surprise. Then understanding dawned in Coal's eyes before he rolled away.

With Geric gone, Haline ran towards the dragon, dagger in hand, and plunged it into the creature's belly. After three deep, hard stabs, she withdrew her knife and stepped away.

The dragon landed and snarled at Haline and Geric, forgetting about Coal. Its wings flapped incessantly as if it was trying to fly away, but then it seemed to lose all of its energy. Suddenly quiet, its anger dissipated, and it lay down on its tattered belly with ragged, wet breaths.

Once he was sure it wasn't going to move, Coal hopped off the dragon. It stared at Coal through one weary, tired eye before it stopped wheezing altogether. Coal studied the camp. No one had noticed their fight because there were countless other battles everywhere else.

Coal walked back towards Haline. Geric sat on the ground cradling his arm while Haline stood over him.

"Haline," Geric said, "what are you doing here?"

"I'm rescuing you." Haline narrowed her eyes. "Why aren't you guarded, and where are Astra and Elizabeth?"

"Just look around. It's chaos everywhere. I don't know where my guard is." Geric glanced nervously at the dilapidated camp.

"This is why you should be guarded." She stepped closer to him. "You snake. You turned them in, didn't you?"

"No, I was caught, just like they were." He looked to Coal for confirmation.

"I didn't see you after Chalcedony found us. I only saw Astra and Elizabeth," Coal said.

Geric gave Coal a cold, hard stare before he softened and focused on Haline. "Just because he didn't see me doesn't mean I wasn't captured."

"You're lying." She sniffed the air. "I can smell the lie on you."

He licked his lips and raised his hands. "I was only protecting you and everything we've worked for."

"By giving them up!" Haline accused.

"They would have found them anyway. Princess Chalcedony isn't stupid. There is no way two kids could have made it to the human realm."

A dragon advanced from above and tried to grab Haline. She stabbed it with her dagger as if she was batting away a fly. It shrieked and flew away. Haline faced Geric once again. Her eyes were hard with anger. "You betrayed me. You promised to get them home."

"I'm sorry." He grabbed her arm. "I didn't think this through."

She pushed him away, trembling.

"Haline," Coal eyed the camp. "We need to find Astra and Lizzy."

"This won't take long." She jumped towards Geric. He tried to move out of her way, but he was a second too slow. Haline ended up on top of him with her dagger to his throat, breathless and grinning. Geric held her wrist, trying to prevent the knife from making contact.

"I'm sorry." Geric's voice shook.

She moved the dagger upwards. Not expecting the change in direction, Geric lost his grip on the knife. With a glint of madness in her eyes, she plunged the knife towards Geric. Coal, reacting on instinct, grabbed her hand before the blade connected with flesh.

Geric narrowed his eyes, in shock rather than in fear. "You would kill me for them?"

She shook away Coal's hand. "Stay out of this."

"I can't let you kill him," Coal said.

Haline snickered. "I'm not going to kill him." She turned to Geric. "I'll let you live if you tell me where Astra and Lizzy are."

"You don't have to threaten me for information. I would have told you regardless." He motioned to a tent halfway across the camp. "They're right there."

If Coal had thought a little harder, he would have been able to pick out Astra and Elizabeth's tent. It was the only tent surrounded by five soldiers. Chalcedony obviously hadn't trusted Astra.

Before Coal could intervene, Haline took her dagger to the side of Geric's face and sliced his ear off. She stood above the dwarf with it in her hand, chuckling.

Geric screamed and scrambled to his feet, holding the spot where his ear should have been. Blood seeped through his fingers and down the side of his face. "You're crazy!"

"You knew that when you hired me, and you knew that before we started dating." She put the ear underneath her breastplate. Even in the darkness Coal saw the smeared blood the ear had left on her breast. "Next time you cross me, I'll kill you."

Geric grimaced before he ran away into the forest.

"Why did you do that?" Coal asked. "He'd already told us where Astra and Lizzy were."

"I don't take betrayal very well." Haline smiled mischievously, and Coal wondered what he'd gotten himself into.

Chalcedony woke from a dreamless sleep wide awake, knowing something was wrong. Then, she heard the snarls.

"What's going on?" Chalcedony shouted at Mahala and Jin.

"There is some disturbance coming from the dragon's nest, Princess!" Jin yelled into the tent. Chalcedony jumped from her cot and dressed. She placed her mother's sword at her back and strapped Mischief to her waist before she left her tent and headed towards the dragon's makeshift nest with her guards at her side.

"Is there something wrong, Princess?" Mahala asked, her gaunt skin glowing in the night.

"That's what I'm going to find out." They stopped in their tracks when three dragons landed on a tent a few yards away. Screams and shouts of surprise came from the fallen tent. Soldiers still in their nightclothes ran out of the tent screaming. Chalcedony ran towards the dragons, her mother's sword drawn.

As she cut through the hide of the closest beast, Mayhem's joy swept through her. She killed the other two before either realized they were being attacked.

"Thank you, Princess," one of the soldiers said.

"Don't thank me. Get your weapons and find out what the hell is going on."

The dragonkeeper had managed to get mostly dressed. Anton wore a halfway buttoned shirt and bed slippers while he barked orders to the few dragon riders that were there.

"Anton, what the hell is going on?" Chalcedony asked.

"Princess!" he exclaimed. "Somehow my dragons have gotten out."

"I can see that!" Chalcedony snapped. "How did this happen?"

"Uh … Someone let them out and covered the tents with carrion."

She hated dragons. They were unpredictable and hostile. Separated, they were docile, but too many in one place and they took on a mob mentality if left unchecked.

She turned to Madoc's personal watchdogs. "Go look for any intruders. Pay special attention to anything that looks out of place."

"We have been assigned to you and you alone," Jin said in a deep, flat voice.

"I understand your dilemma," Chalcedony began. "You fear Madoc's wrath if anything happens to me. But you fail to see the danger in front of you. Disobey me and I will make your lives unbearable."

They were twin soldiers. They fought similarly to how she fought with Avonnah and Djamel—shadowing each other. One never did anything without the other knowing or sensing it. Right now, they were debating her order silently between each other.

Chalcedony punched Mahala in the middle of her chest. The impact sent waves of pain through Chalcedony's hand, but she bottled it up. Before Jin reacted, Chalcedony stepped behind him and had her sword at his neck. After a few uneven breaths, Mahala recovered. She reached for her sword, but when she saw her partner, she stopped.

"You would move against me?" Chalcedony registered Mayhem's pleasure as she held it at Jin's throat. Normally, the thought of hurting her fey was sickening, but the sword had no such qualms. Besides, she resented having them around. They made her feel as if she couldn't defend herself.

"Of course not." Mahala lowered her sword and bent on one knee.

"Stand up," Chalcedony ordered. When Mahala stood, Chalcedony continued. "Who do you follow, me or Madoc?"

"You, Princess," Mahala answered.

"I need both of you to do as I say without hesitation. I won't kill my own, but I will have you discharged and exiled. I won't have anyone with me who will not obey me. Is that understood?"

Jin, who had been rigid in Chalcedony's arms, spoke, "Yes, Princess."

Chalcedony released Jin. "Now, go look for the intruders."

Respect finally registered in Jin and Mahala's eyes. "Yes, Princess."

Madoc's Rule Number Fifteen: Fear Breeds Respect.

Out of the corner of her eye, she saw a soldier fighting to corral one of the dragons. She walked towards the dragon and cut off its head.

Anton gasped and ran towards the decapitated dragon. "Why did you kill it?" he asked incredulously.

"It just attacked one of my soldiers—one of your riders."

"But … we need them."

"Then control them. If you don't, I will kill every single one of them."

Then she saw it: Coal's tent. It lay on the ground completely destroyed. "Damn." Chalcedony faced Anton. "Get these dragons under control."

She tried to run towards his tent, but Mayhem chose that moment to reject Chalcedony. Hands and legs shaking, she returned Mayhem to its sheath on her back. The world spun around her. Frowning, she swallowed the bile rising from her stomach.

"How are we going to get in there?" Coal and Haline were hiding behind a tent a few yards away from Astra and Elizabeth's tent. The image of Haline slicing Geric's ear kept replaying in his head. He'd thought Haline might be crazy when he'd first met her and she'd knocked him unconscious. He'd figured she was borderline crazy when she'd knocked Djamel out. He understood why she'd done both those things. But there was no reason for Haline to sever Geric's ear. She was, without a doubt, crazy.

"The two of us can easily take them," Haline said, tearing Coal away from his thoughts.

"How?"

"We both have weapons. What more do we need?" Haline stalked towards the tent and Coal followed, trying to tamp down his fear.

Before they were halfway there, Astra bolted out of the tent with Elizabeth on her back. Three of the soldiers standing in front of the tent crashed to the ground, never getting a chance to draw their weapons. Coal stared in amazement as Astra sped past. His eyes locked onto Elizabeth as she clutched the spidren's neck.

"Astra!" Elizabeth shouted. "We just passed Coal."

Astra skidded to a stop, giving the remaining soldiers a chance to catch up to them. Astra shot webbing at them. The sticky, thin fabric hit three soldiers, sealing them together. Two more soldiers walked cautiously towards Astra.

With Elizabeth still on her back, Astra jumped on the soldier in front of her. She clamped down on the side of his face. The soldier struggled, and then, abruptly, he stopped moving. His eyes were wide open, darting back and forth, but every other part of his body stayed unnaturally still.

The other soldier made her move as soon as her partner was attacked, but she was too focused on the spidren to notice the other threat. Haline ran her down from behind, grabbed her hair, and hit her forehead into the ground until the soldier stopped moving.

With the moment of nausea gone, Chalcedony took in all of the chaos. Three of her soldiers lay on the ground wrapped in a spider's web. Jin and Mahala were unconscious. And Coal … Coal was running into the forest.

This is not possible. This is not happening.

Chalcedony ran after him, using every bit of energy she had. He turned just as she tackled him to the ground.

"What the hell are you doing?" she demanded.

"I have to take her home, Chaley," he answered, looking up at her, nearly breathless. "She needs her parents."

"You're not going anywhere." She stood and grabbed his arms to force him to his feet. Then, as if he were booby-trapped, she found herself immobile. The spidren stood a few feet from her, pieces of webbing dragging from its abdomen and Elizabeth clinging to its neck.

"I knew I should have killed you when I had a chance!" Chalcedony screamed. "Coal, get me out of here." She tried to wiggle her sword out of its sheath, but her arms were useless. "We had an agreement."

146

"What agreement?" asked a blonde female dwarf with huge cleavage. Haline. This must be the dwarf Geric had told her about.

Coal looked from Chalcedony to Haline. "Chaley said she'd take Lizzy home."

Haline concentrated on Chalcedony and narrowed her eyes. "Really, Princess? When were you planning on doing that?"

Why was this dwarf helping them? What did she have to gain?

"She told me we'd take Lizzy home when the door is back in Everleaf," Coal answered.

"Lizzy, do you want to stay here for three more months?" Haline asked.

"No." The child shook her head eagerly from atop the giant spider.

"So what is it going to be, Coal? Are you going to turn Lizzy over to the bitchy princess or are we going to take her to Queen Isis's land so she can be home in a couple of days?"

"I can take her to another door," Chalcedony said through gritted teeth.

"No, she won't. She will keep Lizzy here to save face. She's been outsmarted and outmaneuvered by two human children. She has no choice but to punish both of you," Haline said.

"And a dwarf," Chalcedony added, glaring at Haline. "I've been attacked by two human children, a dwarf, and a spidren, and you will all be punished."

The dwarf laughed. "You'll have to find us first."

"Coal, who are you going to trust? Them, or your best friend?" Chalcedony yelled, her face red with rage. Coal glanced at Haline and Elizabeth and then back to Chalcedony.

"I have to take her home, Chaley. We never should have taken her."

Chalcedony screamed, trying her best to escape from the web. But then Astra shot webbing at her mouth and her screaming stopped, but it couldn't stifle the hatred and anger in her eyes.

"She's mad," Astra hissed.

"She's beyond mad. She's livid," Haline said, laughing.

Chalcedony started a new thread of muffled screams as Haline approached. "Isn't this your sword?" Haline unbuckled the hilt from Chalcedony's waist, dodging all of Chalcedony's kicks and thrusts.

"It's not really mine." Coal felt guilty seeing Chalcedony lying powerless and frustrated on the ground. "I took it from Chalcedony."

"There is hope for you yet," Haline said. "Take it. You've already stolen it once. You need a weapon, and you're already familiar with this one."

He should have said no, placed it on the ground next to Chalcedony, and walked away. Things were bad enough without Coal taking her sword again, but she had her mother's sword now.

"I'm sorry, Chaley." Coal bent and whispered in her ear. "I'll bring it back. I promise."

She jerked her head towards Coal, barely missing him.

"I promise." He walked away from Chalcedony and back towards Astra and Elizabeth, knowing his words meant nothing to her.

Elizabeth had dismounted and her arms were wrapped tightly around Astra when he reached them.

"Thank you for letting me ride on your back," Elizabeth said once they separated.

"My pleasure, young warrior." Astra turned to Haline and Coal. "Be careful. As soon as your princess is loose she'll come after you. I don't think she'll care anymore if either of you are hurt. She'll be out for your blood." The spidren was as docile as a sprite again.

Haline rubbed Astra's head. "Don't worry about us. The queenling doesn't scare me."

"Goodbye," Astra said before she sped away, blending into the night.

"Snap out of it, boy," Haline said to Coal. "Let's go."

Coal followed Haline and Elizabeth deeper into the forest. A few minutes later, they came upon two napping dragons tied to a tree. They were oblivious to their brethren who were causing chaos just a few yards away.

"What are these here for?" Coal asked.

"Our escape," Haline said.

"Why aren't we taking the tunnels?"

"Chalcedony and her crew know about the tunnels." Haline untied the dragons from the tree. "Have you ridden on one of these before?"

"Yes, a long time ago." He had traveled a few times with Chalcedony. It had been scary and exhilarating, but they had maimed too many handlers in Legacy for him to trust them.

"I used to tame dragons. They are nice once they trust you. Isn't that right?" Haline stroked the back of one of the dragons. To Coal's surprise, it leaned into her touch as if it were a dog.

"Lizzy, do you want to ride with me or Coal?" Haline asked.

"You." Elizabeth released Coal's hand and ran to Haline. He couldn't blame Elizabeth. At least Haline knew what she was doing.

"Coal, you have the smallest dragon."

Coal nodded, hoping the smallest meant the most docile. Haline petted the dragon and talked to it soothingly while Coal mounted.

Haline hefted Elizabeth up onto their dragon and then climbed up front. Without any hesitation, she pulled her reins and they were in the air. Haline circled low and nodded to Coal. He lifted the reins, but the dragon didn't move.

"You have to do it with more balls than that if you want it to move," Haline said from above.

Finding his courage, he pulled the reins tighter and the dragon took flight.

CHAPTER FIFTEEN

The clouds floated peacefully across the moon as Chalcedony lay immobile, restrained, and powerless, wrapped in the spidren's webbing

"Princess?" A haggard face covered in with dried blood and dirt blocked her once mockingly serene view. He leaned closer. "Are you alright, Princess?"

Through the moonlight, Chalcedony saw it was Djamel. He was covered in earth and blood. He looked as though he'd been tortured and then, buried alive, but he was asking her if she was alright. She laughed at the irony and then gagged on the web covering her mouth.

Djamel unsheathed a knife from his boot and cut away the webbing from her mouth and torso.

"Are you okay, Princess?" he asked again.

Chalcedony sat up. "They escaped, Djamel. They outmaneuvered me. I've spent my entire life studying how to be a great leader, and look at us. Our own dragons destroyed our camp. I should just let Madoc rule," Chalcedony said in one hysterical breath as she wiped tears away.

"A male can't rule," he said automatically. Like every male, he'd been taught to stay in his place and never question the rules.

"He has been," Chalcedony whined. "I'm nothing but a child."

Djamel picked her up and pushed her towards the closest tree. She cried out in pain as the rough edges of the bark cut into her back.

"What are you doing?" she asked, too surprised to continue crying.

"If you believe you are a failure, then you are."

"They're gone, Djamel." She wanted to curl up in a ball, shut out the world, and forget about her responsibilities and her failures.

"If anyone is to blame for the humans escaping, it's us. There has been peace for so long that we don't know how to fight as a unit." He looked away, hurt by the memory. He let her go and lowered his head. "I have failed you. We have all failed you."

It was one thing for her to give up, but Djamel giving up felt wrong. "Be quiet, Djamel. We can't both sit here and have a pity party."

The sun peeked over the horizon as Coal's dragon zigzagged through the air. Twice he'd thought they were going to fall, but the dragon would find some reserve energy and correct its course. To Coal's relief, Haline's dragon lost altitude and landed in a meadow full of wildflowers. Butterflies, bees, and other flying bugs hovered over the colorful foliage.

Coal dismounted and stretched his back and legs. Although blood had completely soaked the makeshift bandage covering his hand, it had stopped bleeding a few miles back, and the painful throbbing had died down to a mild ache.

His dragon sniffed the air and set its eyes on the bloody rag wrapped around his hand. It snapped at Coal. Barely avoiding the beast's jaws, Coal fell backward.

"Get back." Haline stepped between Coal and the dragon and stomped her foot. She didn't have a weapon, but the dragon cowered and backed away.

"They're hungry, and it smelled blood." Haline returned to Elizabeth and their dragon. She took off its saddle and pushed the animal into the forest.

"Are we in Queen Isis's land?" Elizabeth asked. During the flight, she'd lost her hair tie, and she kept pushing strands of hair out of her face.

"No, but the dragons are hungry and tired. If we keep riding, they're going to throw us."

Leaving the dragons on their own, the trio set off continued on foot. While they trekked through the trees, Haline taught them which plants were safe to eat and which were dangerous. In the middle of her lesson, Haline fell to the ground with a muffled scream. The shaft of an arrow stuck out of her leg.

Elizabeth screamed as if she had been the one impaled. Coal stepped towards them, but an arrow streaked past his face, stopping him where he stood.

Chalcedony's voice erupted from the forest. "Do not take another step, Coal, or you will be next."

When he saw the anguish on Haline's face, he moved anyway, an arrow released from within the forest landed by his foot.

Elizabeth sobbed as she knelt beside Haline. "Coal, are you okay?"

"I'm fine, Lizzy. It didn't touch me." Coal turned in the direction of Chalcedony's voice. "Haline needs a healer."

Chalcedony and three of her soldiers stepped from the trees directly in front of them. "She'll get one."

"How did you find us so fast?" Haline asked, jaw clenched in pain.

"You didn't scare away all of the dragons. Pick her up," she told Avonnah. "Let's go."

"Princess Chalcedony, you have entered my land without an invitation and then you shoot one of my citizens. That is clearly an act of war."

Someone dropped out of the tree, blocking Avonnah's path. A human, Coal realized when he saw the man's ears.

"Haline." The man bowed as if he didn't see the arrow in her leg. He faced Chalcedony. "Princess, why are you here?"

Chalcedony straightened. "Royden, you have no power here."

"I am Queen Isis's shadow, and I have been granted the power to patrol her land and enforce her laws." The man had tanned, almost brown, skin with eyes the color of murky brown clay.

Chalcedony pulled Avonnah back and confronted Royden. "You're human, and have no power. You can't be a shadow."

"I may not possess magic, but I do have power." He cleared his throat and approximately fifty human and elven soldiers stepped from the forest. From the surprise on her face, Coal knew Chalcedony had had no idea they'd been there any more than he had.

Royden continued. "The dwarf and the humans are guests of Queen Isis. You are unjustly persecuting them."

Chalcedony stepped to him. "You would risk war with me over these humans?"

"You would risk war with my queen?" Royden stepped closer, looking up at her. She towered over him, but he didn't care about the difference in their height. "You are a child. Go home. When you are older perhaps you can return and teach me a lesson."

Like a predator debating on whether to attack or retreat, her gaze darted to Royden before they settled once again on Coal and Elizabeth. "Coal, are you sure this is what you want?"

"Chaley, Lizzy doesn't belong here. I have to take her home."

Chalcedony clenched her fists. "I told you I would take her home!"

"Leave, Princess. The boy refused your offer," Royden said.

She took a deep breath and then sighed noisily before she stalked back into the forest. Her soldiers hesitated for a moment and then followed.

Haline's low grunt drew Coal's attention away from where Chalcedony had disappeared. He ran to her. The arrow had completely pierced her right leg and the leaves underneath were stained red from blood.

"Should we pull it out?" he asked Haline as he knelt beside her.

She shook her head—no—eyes closed, face strained.

"What do you want me to do?" Coal asked.

Royden bent down. "That looks painful, Haline."

She opened her eyes. "What game are you playing, Royden?" Her brows were pinched in pain.

"You're lying on the ground in the middle of a forest with an arrow stuck in your leg. You were about to get thrown to the weavers. You can be damn sure that what I have planned is better than what princess-stick-in-the-mud had planned."

She squinted through her pain. "What do you want? I can take care of this myself."

"Stop being stupid, and let me help. I can get the arrow out, and I can help get these children home."

"Don't go near those children!" she shouted.

Royden cocked an eyebrow. "We are going to the same place, Haline."

"Why are you even here?" She breathed in rapid uneven breaths.

"Two human children defying fey royalty. How could I not come?"

"You need help, Haline," Coal interjected.

"Please," Elizabeth pleaded. "Let him help you."

She took a deep breath. "Fine."

"We're going to have to cut the arrow to get it out of your leg. It'll be better if we do it back in town. My doctor will give you something for the pain."

Haline nodded and didn't argue when a man inserted a needle into her arm.

"The convenience of human medicine is good for something, aye?" Royden ran a hand through his dark brown hair.

"Shut up and get me out of here."

He faced his soldiers. "You heard the lady."

Four of Royden's soldiers lifted Haline and walked into the forest. Coal and Elizabeth followed, but stopped abruptly when Royden blocked their path. "By the way, I'm Royden, Queen Isis's shadow. There's a wagon waiting not far from here."

"I'm Coal, and this is Elizabeth."

"It's nice to meet you." Royden grabbed Coal's undamaged hand for a long, uncomfortable moment. "You're a beautiful boy."

"Thank you." Coal shook his hand free, feeling embarrassed.

"Your hand's hurt, Royden said, noticing the bandage on Coal's wrapped palm. "I'll have our doctor give you something for it." He gave Coal a pat on the shoulder before he walked away.

Coal stared at his bandaged hand and wondered why the man had acted as if he'd found a long-lost friend.

The wagon bounced and shook over the bumpy road taking them to Queen Isis's land. The jostling didn't bother Elizabeth, she dozed silently with her head resting on Coal's lap.

"What you're doing is brave," Royden said, sitting across from Coal and Elizabeth while Haline slept on a cot in the middle of the wagon.

Coal shrugged and tucked a strand of raven colored hair behind Elizabeth's ear.

Royden continued. "Two children escaping from the evil princess. It's inspiring."

"Chalcedony isn't evil. She's just doing her job." The man's admiration made Coal uncomfortable.

"You love her." Royden leaned back. "Love makes bitches of us all. But it's one thing to love and obey. It's another to love and do what's right. You're doing what's right, and you feel guilty about it. It's admirable."

Coal wanted to insist that he and Chalcedony were just friends, but instead, he asked, "Why are you helping us?"

"Like I said, you're inspiring. But why is the girl in the fey realm? It's forbidden to bring humans here against their will."

"Lizzy wanted to come."

"She wanted to come, huh? Then, she just changed her mind. Imagine that from a child. Don't worry," Royden said. "You're doing what's right. It's a horrible thing to send a child to the weavers." Royden grinned. "How do you think Chalcedony looks now that the two of you have escaped?"

Choosing not to answer the question, Coal leaned back and closed his eyes, hoping Royden would take the hint and leave him alone.

Coal patted Elizabeth gently on the shoulder. "Wake up. We're here."

Elizabeth sat up, wide-eyed and alert.

Royden stood outside the wagon, with a hand extended, waiting to help them step down. Elizabeth looked from Coal to Royden and then back to Coal.

"You go first," Coal said. "I'll be right behind you."

Once Elizabeth was on the ground, he followed.

"Are we in the human realm?" Elizabeth asked.

"No. This is Selene, the most beautiful land in all of the Fey Realm, and right now, you are standing in front of Queen Isis's home." Royden's face was lit up with pride.

Queen Isis's house was built with brick and concrete, and it was unlike anything Coal had ever seen in the fey realm. "This is your queen's house?" Coal asked, unable to fathom a queen living in a human dwelling. No wonder Elizabeth had thought she was home.

"Yes, I built it myself," Royden said.

"Why would you want this instead of a tree?" Coal asked. "Trees warn you if there are invaders."

"Humans have amazing ways of protecting their homes without the use of magical trees," Royden retorted.

Coal shrugged and followed Haline as Royden's men carried her out of the wagon. The doctor, who had been walking beside the stretcher, put a hand on Coal's chest to stop him. The doctor had icy blue eyes and patches of blonde hair above his ears. "We need to extract the arrow. You'll only be a distraction."

Coal tried to step past the healer. "I need to make sure she's okay."

Royden grabbed Coal's shoulder and pulled him away from the stretcher. "You can trust Dr. Jold. He's not out to hurt her."

"If we were," Dr. Jold said, "do you really think you could do anything about it?"

Coal shook himself free from Royden's grip and shoved the doctor.

Dr. Jold stepped back. Coal pushed the doctor again, and this time Coal saw fear in his eyes. Good. That's what he was looking for. "If you hurt her, I'll hunt you down and kill you."

He owed Haline. The dwarf was crazy, but she'd gone out of her way to help him and Elizabeth.

Royden stepped between Coal and the doctor. "Jold is an ass, but he's good. She'll be fine. Apologize to our guest, Doctor."

"I apologize." The doctor said, rubbing his chest. "I better go so I can take care of her."

"He is skilled and loyal. I promise you, Haline will be treated like royalty."

Coal watched the doctor walk away and fought the urge to follow. Elizabeth stepped next to him and grabbed his hand.

"Relax," Royden repeated, patting Coal on the back. "Let's go meet my queen."

Royden entered the house, opened his arms wide, and said, "Honey, I'm home."

A short, curvy elf ran toward Royden, wrapped her arms around his neck and gave him a deep, long kiss. Coal watched amazed. He had never seen a human and a fey together.

"Coal and Lizzy, meet Queen Isis," Royden said after they separated.

"It's nice to meet you both," Queen Isis said. Her glossy black hair was streaked with red, and her teeth were even and straight. They weren't sharp like Chalcedony's and the other elves he knew. She wore jeans like Coal had worn to the human realm. If it weren't for her pointy ears and red eyes, she'd look completely human.

Coal stopped gaping and bowed. Elizabeth was about to bow, but Queen Isis stopped her. "You guys don't have to bow to me. I'd be honored to shake your hand."

Elizabeth didn't hide behind Coal like she'd done with Royden, but she didn't take Queen Isis's hand either.

"She doesn't like meeting new fey," Coal said.

"I wouldn't either if the last time I'd met a fey I was taken away from my home." Queen Isis bent on one knee and took Elizabeth's hand. "I promise Royden and I will help get you back home."

Elizabeth nodded and gave Isis the first smile Coal had seen from her since Haline had been shot.

"You have a beautiful smile, Lizzy," Queen Isis said, making Lizzy grin wider. "Let me show you where your rooms are?"

"Yes," Elizabeth said.

"Wait. We need to make the rest of the journey to the door. It opens tomorrow night."

"I am not Chalcedony. I let my people travel freely from this realm to the other. Everyone here knows where it is."

"At every opening, there is a large party with travelers and their families. Believe me, you won't miss it," Royden said.

"It's against the treaty to let humans and fey travel between the realms," Coal replied.

Queen Isis and Royden exchanged a look before Queen Isis said, "I didn't sign the treaty. As long as we behave ourselves, I don't see why we can't go there. For that matter, I don't understand why the realms are separated."

"Humans and their technology don't mix well with fey and our magic," Coal said.

Royden cocked an eyebrow. "Our magic?"

Coal fidgeted. "Well … magic."

Elizabeth yawned.

"Sleep tonight, Coal," Queen Isis said. "I promise Royden will show you to the door tomorrow."

Baby dolls with pale skin, blonde hair and blue eyes covered the bed the room designated for Elizabeth. Queen Isis beamed with. "As soon as I heard you were coming, I had it decorated for you. What do you think?"

A large teddy bear sat in the corner of the room with half a dozen smaller bears surrounding it.

Lizzy shrugged. "It's okay."

Queen Isis frowned, but then it quickly disappeared as she turned to Coal. "Your room is right next door. I'll show you."

"No. We're not being separated," Coal said.

"Since you're a boy, I thought it—"

"We're not separating," Coal repeated. He was in charge of Elizabeth now. Like Haline, he wasn't sure if he trusted Queen Isis and Royden.

"I understand. I wasn't thinking about it from your point of view," Queen Isis said. "Okay, I'll leave both of you alone to rest."

"She's pretty, huh?" Elizabeth asked Coal once they were alone in the overwhelmingly pink room.

"Yes," Coal answered.

"I'm glad she's a queen and not a princess like Chalcedony. I don't like princesses."

"They aren't that bad, Lizzy." He yawned and lay on the bed. "Go to sleep. We'll go check on Haline tomorrow and then, you're going home."

She snuggled next to him.

"I wish I were home now," she said in a low, sleepy voice.

"Me, too," Coal said, wondering if he'd ever be able to return to Legacy.

CHAPTER SIXTEEN

Chalcedony sat cross-legged in the grass in front of a small pond. She imagined she looked patient and calm, but that was the opposite of how she felt. Madoc had used a dragon and flown to the edge of Queen Isis's land as soon as he'd heard Coal and Elizabeth had escaped … again. He'd been lecturing her for the past fifteen minutes. Normally, they would be indoors so her soldiers could pretend not to hear her getting scolded, but she hadn't bothered to set up camp since the dragons had destroyed most of the tents.

"I think you're failing on purpose," Madoc accused. "You don't want to succeed because when you do, you'll have to punish them."

Chalcedony stood. She had been taking her reprimand calmly until then. He hadn't said anything she hadn't already berated herself for, but accusing her of letting Coal escape on purpose crossed the line.

"I would never waste time and risk the lives of my soldiers on something I didn't plan on winning and seeing through to the end. Listen up!" Chalcedony shouted, although she knew everyone was already listening. "Does anyone feel like I have been too soft on Coal and Elizabeth?" After no one spoke, she said, "There will be no repercussions for being honest. In fact, I need the criticism. What am I doing wrong?"

"Princess, you've worked hard to track down those children. The humans just seem to have luck on their side," Jin said. He had been appointed by Madoc, but Chalcedony and the entire army knew he was really there to spy on her. It felt good to hear him speak on her behalf.

"Is this how everyone feels?" Chalcedony asked. "We've been unlucky?

"Luck. Is that what wins battles?" Chalcedony paced in front of the soldiers, raising her voice. "I refuse to believe that luck determines winners. What about skill and determination? Coal's allies have all of these qualities. I refuse to admit defeat based on luck. I refuse to accept they are smarter, more skilled, or more determined than we are."

Chalcedony stopped pacing. "I should have told you this from the beginning. If I had, maybe everyone would have fought harder. Yes, Elizabeth broke a law. But it was never my intention to harm her. No one would have been permitted to touch her. Before I could prove that, Coal took Elizabeth. And he's made her endure much worse than she would have if she'd stayed."

Chalcedony stalked back to Madoc. She stopped beside the expressionless advisor and said in a low voice, "If you ever accuse me of risking fey lives and failing on purpose, you'll be spending the rest of your life in a dark, dank box underground."

As soon as rays of light peeked through the concrete-encased windows, Coal woke Elizabeth, they got dressed, and he ushered her out of the room with the promise of finding Haline.

He expected the hallway to be empty, but Royden stood across from them wearing a pair of jeans and a white T-shirt. "Good morning," he said.

"How did you know we were awake?" Coal asked, feeling as if he were being watched.

"I didn't think you'd sleep long." His tone was light and easy, like he'd never had a bad day in his life. "I have made it my life's mission to serve you until you and the girl make it home."

Elizabeth and Coal exchanged a look of apprehension. Then, Elizabeth said, "We want to see Haline."

"Of course. I'll show you the way."

"Why is it so quiet here?" Coal asked. The halls of Legacy were always loud and bustling with ambassadors and their staff, but this place was immaculate and empty.

Royden shrugged. "It's not that it's quiet here. It's just crowded in Princess Chalcedony's tree with diplomats, servants, birds, squirrels and all. Your princess and Madoc try their best to rule everyone. We trust them to rule themselves."

Coal noticed he said "we" as if they ruled together. How did he have so much power in a world that looked down on humans?

"This is it." Royden stopped at a door on the other side of the house. He tapped lightly on the door and entered without waiting for a response. Haline sat on the bed with her leg propped on pillows. Strips of brown cloth were wrapped around her injured leg and most of her foot.

She'd been eating before they entered. She chewed, swallowed, said, "Good morning," before she scowled at Royden.

"Good morning to you also, Haline." Royden turned to Coal. "I'll give you some space."

Once he'd left, Haline said, "The less time you spend with him and that queen, the better."

"They're nice." Elizabeth climbed onto Haline's bed and chewed on a piece of toast.

"Trust me," Haline said. "Something is wrong with them."

"But they let humans in their lands freely," Coal said, "and they're helping us."

"What's in it for them? They're breaking the treaty. Eventually, they'll get bold and cross it completely. Then what?" Haline scooped some eggs onto her toast. "And Queen Isis is too nice. There's a reason queens are bitches and have countless advisors and ambassadors. They need to know everything. But Royden is Isis's only advisor. Humans can't perform magic, my ass. He's clearly put her under a spell."

Coal liked seeing a human and a fey together. It was impossible for him and Chalcedony, but at least someone had made it work.

Haline peered at Coal with narrowed eyes as if she could read his thoughts. "Don't let him enchant you, too."

"What's in it for you?" Coal asked. "You're helping us."

"You're children. I may be crazy, but I'm not heartless."

"How do you know they aren't trustworthy?" Coal asked.

"Whenever I traveled here to see Geric, we'd visit Royden and Queen Isis. They are too damn happy. That much happiness is impossible." Haline put her tray on the side of the bed and leaned back. "And you saw how trustworthy Geric was."

Haline eyed Coal. "Go eat. I'm sure they have a large breakfast waiting for you."

"When will you be able to walk?" Elizabeth asked.

"The doctor said it shouldn't take long."

"And then we can leave?" Elizabeth asked.

"Then we can leave," Haline answered. "Let me rest, and I'll see you later."

Queen Isis's dining room was small and held no pictures or ornaments on the wall, but the food on the table was far from simple. Delicacies from the entire realm were laid out before them. There were indigo-colored felab berries that tasted like strawberries, but had the texture and shape of bananas. Pamici apples that only ripened once a year and were worth more than a soldier's monthly wage, according to a soldier he'd overheard. Roasted lamb and pheasant with loves of breads and glazed pastries rounded out the feast. With just the four of them, Coal wondered how they were going to eat all of it.

"Have a seat, Coal." Royden motioned to the seat beside him.

"I'm not hungry. Can you show me where the door is?" As good as the food looked, he had a mission, and he didn't want to get distracted.

"Now?" Royden asked. "It doesn't open until sunset."

"I'd feel better knowing where it was."

"I'm hungry. I want to stay and eat." Elizabeth said, munching on a piece of fruit.

"Go ahead, babe," Queen Isis said. "I'll keep Elizabeth busy."

"Lizzy, do you want to come?" Coal cocked an eyebrow and silently begged her to say yes. She shook her head and placed a pamici apple on her plate. Evidently, she had decided to trust Queen Isis and Royden despite Haline's warning.

Royden stood in front of a miniature car with no doors or windows. "It's called a golf cart. I don't take it out often, but I'm in a mood to show off."

"Chalcedony would have a fit if she saw this."

"Hopefully, she'll never know about it." Royden's tone and his wide grin made it obvious he was looking forward to Chalcedony seeing it. "It uses batteries that I bring over from the human realm every time the door opens."

"I miss cars." Royden said once they were both inside. He pushed a button near the steering wheel and the cart started to move. "Of course, this doesn't go very fast, but it's a nice reminder."

"If you like cars, why are you here instead of the human realm?" Coal asked.

"This place calms me. Whenever I'm in the human realm, I get into trouble. The speed, the unending choices, the technology, the greed, it's all intoxicating. Here, with Isis, it's quiet and simple." He gazed at Coal briefly and then turned back towards the road. "You are the most excitement I've had in a while."

"Are you helping us because it's exciting?"

Royden smiled, the corners of his eyes wrinkled, but he didn't answer the question.

When the cart stopped at the bottom of a large hill, Royden stepped out and said, "This is where the door will open."

Just as with Chalcedony's door, nothing indicated that an entrance to an entirely different world lay ahead.

"Why don't you hide the existence of the door, like Princess Chalcedony?" Coal asked, looking up at the hill.

"The treaty is old. Once, humans were violent and stupid, and they threatened fey, but they have matured. With the discovery of their modern medicine and technology, I know we can live together again."

Coal stared at the hill and thought about how contradictory everything and everyone here seemed compared to Everleaf. What would it have been like, Coal wondered, to live here where humans were accepted?

Coal caught Royden watching him again. "Why do you keep staring at me?"

"You noticed, huh?" The man inhaled deeply, stalling for time. "I had a son. It was just me and him, but my nature attracts trouble or trouble is attracted to me, maybe a lot of both. So, he was taken from me and I was jailed. After my release, I tracked him down. But he seemed happy with the new family they'd placed him with. After my failure, I didn't feel like I had the right to take him from his new home.

"You remind me of him. Innocence and beauty. You have it, and my son had it." Royden's eyes were distant, but he stared directly at Coal. It was the same look Elizabeth's mother had when she watched helplessly as Chalcedony walked away with Elizabeth.

Royden's eyes watered, and he turned away, coughing.

"Sorry. That wasn't very manly of me. This is it," Royden said, his tone less serious and more humorous. "Tonight, this place will become a portal into the human realm, and it'll stay open for three days. Most will leave at dusk when the door opens. But we'll leave tomorrow morning. I've arranged for the vendor who sends my supplies over to meet us on the other side. He'll take you wherever you need to go."

CHAPTER SEVENTEEN

Coal stood on the edge of the festival in nervous awe. Fey and humans filled an entire field outside of town. Because of the cold, everyone wore jackets: reds, whites, blues, and countless other colors, which made it difficult to tell the difference between human and fey. It was as if they were all one multi-hued species, instead of two groups who were supposed to hate and fear each other.

Elizabeth had refused the pink coat Queen Isis had given her. Instead, she wore a black coat that was too big. It had an inside pocket deep enough to hide her dagger. She'd said she wanted to be prepared if Chalcedony came for her. Coal hadn't been as vocal, but he made sure he wore his sword over the back of his coat.

They passed a group of wide-eyed fey and human children sitting in front of a stage. The children watched as human actors shot at each other with fake guns. Everyone greeted Queen Isis and Royden with warm smiles. The friendly greetings were a sharp contrast to Everleaf, where everyone regarded Chalcedony with apprehension and fear.

Before they left the market, Royden stopped at a wooden booth where a giant looked out over bottles of powders and potions. When they approached, the elf behind the booth stopped talking to the giant and straightened up. "Queen Isis, how nice to see you."

"Oliver." Queen Isis was wearing a red coat, and she held a wooden picnic basket on her arm as if it were a pocketbook. "What are you selling?"

"Glamour. Just Glamour." Oliver was a chubby, tall elf with dark circles under his eyes.

Queen Isis stared at the vendor's goods. "Royden."

Royden stepped beside Queen Isis and touched each bottle briefly before he moved to the next. Each time Royden touched one of the bottles, the vendor glanced nervously from it to Royden.

"What is this?" Royden finally asked, picking up the blue vial.

"Glamour." The elf tried to sound impatient, but his voice cracked, ruining the effect.

Royden opened it and sniffed. "What type?"

"Uh …" Oliver cleared his throat. "Well … it's transformation glamour."

"It smells like a transformation potion, not glamour," Royden said.

"That's impossible." With shaking hands, Oliver took the vial from Royden, smelled it, and then laughed nervously. "I have no idea how that got mixed in with the rest." Oliver capped the bottle and was about to put it away when Royden grabbed it.

"Oliver." Queen Isis took the vial from Royden and put it in her coat pocket. "Are you going to make me regret giving you another chance?"

The little bit of color that Oliver had disappeared from his face, although there was no sound of a threat in her voice. She was completely relaxed. "No, Queen Isis. It won't happen again."

She smiled as if it was the best news she'd heard all day. "Good. Stop by and talk to me later. We can catch up."

Oliver didn't relax. He stood completely still. "Yes, maybe once the festival is over."

"Good." Queen Isis turned towards Coal and Elizabeth. "There is an empty spot over there."

"What was that about? Why was he so nervous?" Coal asked as they walked away.

Queen Isis said, "We don't have a night market here, which means we don't have dark magic. Oliver likes to forget that sometimes."

"What's a transformation potion?" Elizabeth asked.

"Glamour is an illusory magic, but the transformation potion can physically change your appearance as if you were a shape shifter. Unfortunately, it kills and disfigures more of its users than it helps."

167

"Magic and potions don't work on me," Elizabeth said with pride.

"We heard rumors," Queen Isis said. "I didn't think they were true. I've never met anyone that was impervious to magic."

"I am. Chalcedony tried to use magic to make me sleep but none of it worked. That's probably why Chalcedony's advisors insisted she send you to the weavers. People will pay an incredible amount of money to become impervious to magic. They wanted to bottle you up and sell you." Royden tickled her, and Elizabeth giggled as she tried to get away.

"If Elizabeth is a magic null, how can she travel through portals?" Coal asked.

Royden said, "Magic nulls can't be manipulated by magic, but they can use magic."

"Here we are." Queen Isis stopped at the last bit of empty grass at the base of the hill and laid out a red and black blanket before she rummaged through the picnic basket. "We can talk about magic nulls later. Right now, I'm starving." She said, "We packed hamburgers for Elizabeth and lamb for you, Coal."

"Hamburgers, really?" Elizabeth asked. "Oh, wow! I've missed these sooo much." She watched impatiently as Queen Isis pulled the food out of the basket. As soon as the food was in front of her, Elizabeth snatched it and took a massive bite.

"And," Queen Isis said, "we brought Butterfingers for dessert."

"What's that?" Coal asked.

"You don't remember them from the human realm?" Royden asked.

"No," Coal said.

Royden grinned and pulled a small yellow package from the picnic basket. "Try this. It's a Butterfinger."

Coal unwrapped the bar and bit into it. It was hard, but with a little pressure it gave way. The delicious sweetness coated his tongue. For a moment, he remembered his childhood in the human realm. Tall brick buildings loomed in the background as he ran in circles with a red ball while a woman with light brown skin watched him from afar.

"I think … I think I remember these." Coal had never had a memory of anyone he'd known from the human realm before. His throat tightened, and he longed for a woman he didn't know.

"Tastes and smells can awaken old memories," Queen Isis said.

Coal hesitated, mouth suddenly dry. "I saw a woman."

"Was she your mother?" Elizabeth asked, wide-eyed and expectant.

"I don't remember my mother. I was homeless when Chalcedony found me."

"Who told you that?" Royden asked.

"Chalcedony."

"Considering the source, you may have cause to doubt her."

"She wouldn't lie to me about my mother," Coal said, knowing the truth in his bones. He didn't have a mother. It was a fact he'd built his life on. Coal knew Royden wanted to say something more against Chalcedony. They didn't understand why he defended her, but without her, he had no idea how his life would have turned out.

"Oh, wow!" Elizabeth interjected, interrupting the uncomfortable silence. "They have a Gameboy."

"What?" Coal asked.

"Video games," Elizabeth mumbled with a mouth full of food. "Can I go play with them?" she asked after she swallowed.

"Is it safe?" Coal asked.

"Everyone knows the rules here. It's safe," Royden said. "The only thing she has to worry about is Chalcedony, and she isn't here."

"Okay then. Bye!" Before Coal objected, Elizabeth ran away and joined a bunch of kids huddled in a circle a few yards away.

"Royden," chirped a device clipped onto Royden's pants. Both he and Queen Isis carried them on their waist. Royden hesitated for a moment and then it chirped again. Finally, he pulled it from his hip. "What's up?"

"You're not going to believe this," a female voice crackled through the device. "The queenling and her army are heading this way."

Royden sat up, suddenly tense. "I thought she was headed back home."

"Apparently, she changed her mind."

"I'll be right there." Royden glanced nervously at Coal before he spoke. "Make sure they don't make it past our borders." He stood and placed it back on his hip. "I have to go."

Queen Isis stood. "You don't think she will risk war over this, do you?"

"No, she won't, but I need to make sure she doesn't cross our borders." Royden turned to Coal, his eyes mostly hidden by the fur lining of his hooded coat. "I have to leave. If I'm not back in the morning, go without me. I promise she won't get past our border."

"Do you want me to phase you there?" Queen Isis asked.

"No, I need soldiers with me in case she's stupid enough to start something. Besides, it won't take long to get there with the horses. Stay here and make sure they make it home," he said.

"I can help." Coal stood. "I'm good with a sword."

"No, your priority is Lizzy. Let me take care of this."

"But they're here for Lizzy and I—"

Royden placed his hand on Coal's shoulder. "I have hundreds of soldiers at my call, but you're the only one that little girl trusts. You need to stay here."

Coal nodded. Royden was right. He needed to get her home. She came first.

"Good." Royden patted Coal's back. It seemed as if he was going to say something else, but he turned towards Queen Isis and gave her a quick kiss before he sprinted away, speaking orders into a device Coal knew to be a hand held radio, a piece of human technology Chalcedony's mother had banned long ago. But it was the was one of the common human tech.

Coal sat back onto the blanket, feeling useless. "I'm sorry that we're putting you through so much trouble."

"You don't need to be sorry." Queen Isis sat next to him on the blanket. "Royden is more than capable of handling Princess Chalcedony. Did Royden tell you about his son?"

Coal looked up, surprised by the question. "Yes."

"Don't feel guilty. You are doing him a favor by allowing him to help. He believes that if he helps you, he'll be atoning for abandoning his child."

"Why doesn't he look for his son?"

"He knows where he is, but Royden doesn't think he'll be forgiven. Would you forgive your parents if they suddenly showed up after they'd abandoned you?"

"I don't know." He thought the longing to have a mother had died, but the desire had awakened when he saw the love and hurt in Deedee's eyes when they left with Elizabeth. She'd diverted her gaze, but not before Coal saw the sadness in her eyes.

"Royden told me you're returning to Everleaf after you take Lizzy home. I know you feel like you have to pay for betraying Princess Chalcedony, but you don't belong with the weavers or in Everleaf. After you take Lizzy home, you should come back here."

"No, I have to make things right with Chalcedony."

Queen Isis grabbed Coal's hand and dug her nails into his palm. "You do not have anything to make up for. She should be apologizing to you and the girl she took."

"Ouch!" Coal pulled his hand away. "What was that for?"

"I know that you care for her, but you need to wake up. Consider this: Royden and I can't have children. We need an heir. Someone strong. Come back here and you can be a prince."

A prince? "That's not possible. I'm human."

"Telling me I can't do something will only make me want to do it more." Queen Isis's eyes sparkled. "Royden and I are going to change the fey realm. Return and help us."

Coal looked out towards the crowd of smiling and laughing fey and humans. Her offer was tempting. Very tempting. But just as he knew he had to take Elizabeth home, he knew he needed to come back and make things right with Chalcedony.

Queen Isis leaned back and asked, "You love her that much?"

"The Chalcedony tracking us is different than the Chalcedony I know."

She shrugged. "I used to be surrounded by advisors and ambassadors who constantly told me what I should do and how I should behave. But, at the end of the day, we all have to do what is right, not what others whisper into our ears.

"I hope you are at least comforted by the fact that you are doing what is right."

"You sound like Royden."

"He's right. Promise me that you will at least think about returning?" Queen Isis asked. "Please?"

Did they really want him? Grigory had offered him a home and an apprenticeship out of pity. But he didn't feel like anyone pitied him here. "I promise I'll think about it."

Chalcedony stood on the border of Queen Isis's land, forcing herself to stay still. When she'd left Coal and Royden in the forest, she'd had every intention of admitting defeat and leaving. But just as she'd reached her destroyed camp, a plan emerged. It was risky and full of holes, but still viable.

She had given her army a choice: stay and fight or go back home. All had eagerly agreed to stay, even though they'd be fighting against a queen.

Her scouts had found a clear, flat piece of land not far from Queen Isis's border, where she could see for miles, so it was no surprise when Royden appeared on the horizon. It looked like his entire army was with him. Good. They were taking her seriously. Her spy had told her that Queen Isis had stayed with Coal and Elizabeth, which worked out perfectly for her. Her army could take a human.

Royden dismounted and walked towards Chalcedony as if he had no other place to be. She estimated that he had two dozen more soldiers than she had, but a quarter of his soldiers were human. That evened the numbers. The strength of numbers had been on his side the last time they'd met. Now, she had almost as many soldiers, and with their numbers being even, she could squash this arrogant human.

Queen Isis had done what Chalcedony would never have had the courage to do: she'd taken on a human lover. And he was ruling beside her like he was as important as any fey. He wasn't. His pride would lose him this battle.

"Princess," Royden said as he approached. "Did you leave something? I thought you were heading home."

"You took something from me. I want it back," Chalcedony said.

"You talk about them as if they were pieces of property."

Damn him. "Technically, they are my property. They are under my protection."

"They came with me willingly." He didn't have the cockiness in his voice like their last encounter when he'd outnumbered her. One-on-one, she knew without a doubt she could best him. By his change in attitude, he knew it too.

"I have my full army with me now, so I ask you again: are you willing to go to war over them?" she asked.

"If standing up for two children means that we go to war, then yes."

"I need to hear that from Queen Isis," Chalcedony said as a formality. She didn't want to see Queen Isis any more than Royden wanted to see Chalcedony.

"I am her shadow," Royden replied as if he'd said it a hundred times. "I speak on her behalf."

"Are you doing this because they are humans like you?" Chalcedony asked, lowering her voice, truly curious.

"I am doing what's right. Why have you brought an entire army to my border to fight for two children that aren't supposed to be in this realm?"

Last night, Chalcedony had asked herself the same question. The answer was simple: Coal. At first, she went after him because she couldn't believe he would leave her. Now, it was vengeance. "He's gotten to you, too, hasn't he?" Chalcedony asked. "He pretends to be honest and loyal, but he will betray you just like he betrayed me."

Royden clicked his tongue at her as if she was a child. She fought the urge to pull out her sword and cut out his tongue.

"He is a charming boy. I am proud to know him, but I'm here because good is worth fighting for. What you're doing is wrong. And if your mother were here, she'd tell you the same."

She recoiled. His words felt like punches to her gut. "How the hell would you know what my mother would do?"

"You have more than a little bit of her in you. She was also self-righteous and stubborn. She kicked me out of the realm more than a few times. I hated her for being so … exacting. I respected her because of her strength and intelligence. She would never have persecuted anyone that didn't deserve it, and she would never risk the lives of her soldiers on selfish pursuits."

Fighting the urge to claw his eyes out, she took a few deep breaths and fought back tears of anger and frustration. She felt heat rising in her cheeks as if she were about to explode. Enough waiting. It was time. Without another word, she stalked back to her soldiers.

Once she reached Djamel and Avonnah on the front line, she said, "Go ahead. Take him down."

The soldiers created a path for her and then closed it, allowing her to disappear within their ranks. She was only halfway through when the sounds of war began. Then she ran, the dead grass giving way beneath her feet. She hated leaving her soldiers to fight alone, but they had their job and she had hers. The sooner she completed her part, the sooner this would be over.

CHAPTER EIGHTEEN

"I saw her!" Elizabeth breathed heavily. Coal had been so distracted by his conversation with Queen Isis that he'd forgotten to check on her.

"You saw who?" Queen Isis stood and rubbed Elizabeth's back in an attempt to calm her.

"Chalcedony. She had a different skin color, but it was her. Queen Isis, please don't let them take us back."

"How do you know it was her if she'd shape-shifted?" Coal asked.

"Her eyes," Elizabeth said, blinking rapidly. "They were still red. I was playing the video game, and when I looked up, I saw her."

Queen Isis took Elizabeth under her arm, embracing her. "I won't let her touch you." She took the device from her waist. "Royden, are you there?"

Royden's voice came through, but he was drowned out by shouting and the sound of fighting.

"Royden!" Queen Isis held onto the device so tightly that her knuckles had gone white. "Royden, what is going on?"

There was only silence as Queen Isis studied the device with exasperation. Elizabeth hung onto Queen Isis as tears fell from her closed eyes. Finally, Royden's voice crackled through the device.

"Babe, what's up? I'm in the middle of something right now."

"They had the nerve to attack? I'll be right there," Queen Isis said.

"No!" Royden shouted. "Make sure the kids make it home. I'll take care of this. I have to go. Get them home, Isis."

Queen Isis glanced nervously at Coal before she spoke. "I'll get them through the door, and then I'll be there to help you."

"Fine, but get them home first!"

Queen Isis placed the device back at her waist. She continued rubbing Elizabeth's back. "Princess Chalcedony won't take you. I promise." Her voice was soft and reassuring, but her eyes were cold. They had changed from soft reddish-brown to a fiery red. "Change of plans, let's get you two to the door now."

"What about Chalcedony?" Coal asked, looking out at the crowd. The sun was setting and everyone had begun crowding around the hill where the door was supposed to be. "How is Chalcedony here when she is supposed to be fighting Royden?"

"She's probably using her army as a distraction," Queen Isis said. "She has no idea who she is messing with." Queen Isis flexed her hand open and closed. "Stupid girl. She would have been better off staying on the border. Royden is much more forgiving than I am."

"Where was she?" Queen Isis asked Elizabeth.

"She was by the market. Where you were talking to that guy for selling bad potions."

"Did she see you?" Coal asked.

"No, she wasn't looking my way." Elizabeth shook her head vigorously. "As soon as I saw her, I walked away so she wouldn't see me."

"That was brave," Queen Isis said. "The door should be opening soon. Let's go. If she says anything to you, she'll regret it."

Coal started to follow, but stopped and grasped Queen Isis's arm. "Wait. We have to get Haline first."

"My priority is getting you two through the door. Haline will be fine."

"No," Coal insisted. "We would never have gotten here without her."

Queen Isis's eyes were hard and fierce. "I don't have time for this. I have to help Royden."

"I'm not abandoning her," Coal repeated.

"Haline is our friend. I don't want to leave her, either." Elizabeth's voice shook.

Coal sighed, thankful that Elizabeth had backed him up. He understood Queen Isis was in a hurry to get them to the door so she could help Royden, but he couldn't leave without Haline.

Still grasping Elizabeth's hand, Queen Isis stomped towards Coal. While she approached, she grew. Coal thought he was imagining things, but she was now a foot taller than him.

"Fine." Queen Isis touched his shoulder. Everything exploded into light. He closed his eyes to shut it out, but the brightness pierced his eyelids. Just as suddenly as it began, the light receded, and he felt the ground underneath his feet.

"How the hell did you get here?"

Coal opened his eyes. Haline was sitting in bed with a book on her lap, her injured leg propped on pillows. Queen Isis had just done what he'd seen Tetrick do to Chalcedony dozens of times: she'd phased with him.

"Haline!" Elizabeth shouted, and ran towards the bed. "We came to get you."

"I see you're finally showing your true self," Haline said to Queen Isis.

Queen Isis removed her hand from Coal's shoulder and glared at Haline. The queen had shrunk a little, but she remained taller and wider than Coal.

"I think you're pretty," Elizabeth said, "and strong. I bet you can beat up Chalcedony's entire army."

Queen Isis's tight-lipped expression cracked into a thin smile. "I get excited and shift uncontrollably. Anyway," she said to Haline, "Chalcedony is here. We need to get them through the door, but they wanted to come and get you first."

"How do you propose to get out of here with me?" Haline pointed to her injured leg.

Coal licked his lips. "I can carry you."

"You can't carry me and watch after Lizzy."

"We have to do something." Coal panicked at the thought of having to do it alone.

"I'm not going. Besides, I never said I was going to the human realm. I only planned to take you to the door. Now, Queen Isis has that job covered. I'm perfectly content with eating Isis's food and abusing her staff until my leg gets better. "

"But—"

"No buts. I can't go," Haline said with a finality Coal knew he couldn't argue with. "Besides, I didn't bring Lizzy here. You did."

Elizabeth rubbed her eyes and said softly, "But you're supposed to show me how to be a warrior."

"Coal knows how to be a soldier. Just do what he tells you."

Elizabeth nodded and gave Haline a hug.

"Alright. Get out of here before Isis explodes." Haline's voice cracked and her eyes were glistening.

"Let's go." Queen Isis's body shrank while she extended her hand to Elizabeth and Coal.

Chalcedony stood next to Tetrick in the heart of Queen Isis's land. She'd reluctantly put aside her pride and asked Tetrick for help. She'd told him her plan, and he'd silently listened without interrupting. After a long pause where she thought he'd say no, he'd agreed to help by phasing away from Queen Isis's border and into the human realm to get Coal and Elizabeth.

She felt like a coward for leaving her soldiers to fight alone, but they knew the plan. As soon as she had Coal and Elizabeth, she'd signal for her army to retreat.

"What is going on, Tetrick?" Chalcedony asked.

"I brought you here instead of straight to the human realm because I wanted to show you this." Tetrick looked out at the large crowd of humans and fey. There were hundreds of humans and fey at the base of the hill of Queen Isis's door, as well as vendors and musicians. "I believe most everyone here is preparing to go through the door. "I have heard Queen Isis was partial to humans," Tetrick said, "but I hadn't heard anything about this."

She inwardly cringed when Tetrick compared her to Queen Isis, but she kept her voice steady. "This must be why patrolling the human realm has become so difficult. She is letting everyone through her door."

Why didn't I know about this? Does Madoc know? She had been so focused on removing the fey from the human realm that she hadn't given much thought to how they were getting there.

They watched as a group of trolls directly in front of them used glamour to appear as humans. Tetrick stepped towards them with a hand on his sword.

Chalcedony grabbed his arm. "Not now. This isn't why we came. And," she stressed, "you're not supposed to be here."

There was a spark of anger in his eyes.

"Why are you helping me, Tetrick?" Chalcedony asked, out of curiosity and to distract him. She had been training with him for two years, but she barely knew him. He never talked about himself.

"My mother thinks that you are not fit to be a queen. But I've trained you. I know that's not true. I want her to eat her words for once, but if anyone finds out I've helped you, even if you succeed, you will lose. The victory would not be considered yours."

Chalcedony didn't know he disliked his mother so much. But how could she? He never talked about anything but patrolling the human realm. If anyone found out that Tetrick had helped bring Coal and Elizabeth back to Legacy, Tetrick would get all of the credit and she'd still be thought of as weak. Weak. Just the thought of the word made her sick to her stomach. Yes, she was cheating, but if Coal could ask for help, why couldn't she?

"When we do find them, it will be almost impossible for me to phase all four of us at once if they don't come willingly," Tetrick said.

"That shouldn't be a problem.," Chalcedony said, "I'll knock them out if I have to."

CHAPTER NINETEEN

"Where do you think Chalcedony is?" Coal asked after Queen Isis had phased them back to the festival.

"I don't have to think." While Coal and Elizabeth watched, Queen Isis's nose grew into the shape of a canine's muzzle. Her eyes turned from blazing red to deep yellow.

With a toothy grin, she sniffed the air. "I can smell her maliciousness from here."

"Wow!" Elizabeth's stared wide-eyed and amazed.

Queen Isis grinned and wiped a bit of saliva from her chin before she transformed her nose and eyes back into their elven shape. "I know exactly where she is."

She motioned towards the back of someone wearing a green coat standing in the middle of the crowd. Unlike Queen Isis, Chalcedony couldn't change her girth or height, so Coal knew her tall, lanky frame the instant he saw it.

"The door should be opening soon. I'm going to take Chalcedony out of the game while you take Elizabeth home. The crowd is large enough. It should be easy for the two of you to blend in." Queen Isis spoke rapidly, her words coming out rushed and almost indecipherable. Her hands shook, and Coal didn't know if it was from apprehension or excitement.

Coal nodded, too nervous to speak.

Queen Isis towered over him. Her fine, shiny black hair, along with her red stripe, lost its gloss and became shaggy like dog hair. Coal realized Queen Isis wasn't apprehensive at all. She was excited, like a wolf anxious for its next kill.

He grasped Queen Isis before she stalked away.

"Don't kill her," Coal said without thinking. His mouth suddenly dry, he felt like he was in the presence of something malicious.

Her eyes sparkled mischievously. "I don't make promises I won't keep."

Coal tightened his grip on Queen Isis's arm. "Please, don't kill her."

She looked at his hand. "You make lots of demands, don't you? I was trying to make you feel comfortable here, but when Royden is in danger, my claws come out." She paused, looking a bit saner. "I can't promise I won't hurt her. But I will promise not to kill her."

Queen Isis shrunk and bent down to Elizabeth.

"It's okay," Elizabeth said. "I'm not scared of you like that."

Queen Isis changed back. "Good. You're a brave soldier." She kissed Elizabeth on the cheek with her muzzle and stood up.

"When I start talking to her," Queen Isis said to Coal, "that's your chance to go through the door, and don't look back. I think she left most of her soldiers on the border, but be prepared in case she brought someone with her."

Coal touched his sword and nodded.

"I've seen enough," Chalcedony said to Tetrick. "Let's go."

"Get your soldiers off my land now," a seething voice said.

Chalcedony turned, her heart pounding. She had met the small and quiet queen at her mother's funeral. Unlike Queen Tasla, she didn't wield her power around like a hammer. But the person Chalcedony had met at the funeral was not the same person standing before her. The power—and anger—emanating from this fey was unimaginable. This was not an elf, but a monster almost as tall as a giant, with the mouth and eyes of a rabid dog. If it was not for Queen Isis's famous red streak in the beast's hair, Chalcedony would not have known who it was.

Chalcedony looked to Tetrick, but he'd already disappeared. He'd told her he wouldn't do anything except phase her here, and true to his word, he was gone. She was in this alone.

"Why are you here instead of helping your soldiers?" Chalcedony asked.

"Did you really think you could sneak into my land and take Coal and the child while no one was looking?"

"Maybe." Chalcedony stepped back. If Queen Isis touched her, she would transport Chalcedony to the border. She needed to keep her distance while she thought of a way out of this.

"You're only a queenling. You can't defeat me." Queen Isis's yellow eyes narrowed. "Call off this stupid, childish war."

"I don't want to fight you," Chalcedony said. "I'm only here for Coal and Lizzy."

"That's not happening," Queen Isis growled.

Chalcedony was about to argue to buy herself more time, but Queen Isis reached for her right shoulder. She leaned back and punched the queen in her jaw. The impact sent a sharp pain up Chalcedony's arm. She hoped the pain was twice as bad for Queen Isis. If it was, Queen Isis didn't register it because a moment later, Queen Isis's foot connected with the side of Chalcedony's head. Lights danced behind her eyelids as she fell to the ground.

Chalcedony's ears rang and she couldn't tell up from down, but she did know she needed to move. She wrapped her arms around her body and rolled twice, ending up on her hands and knees. The group that had surrounded them scampered away before Chalcedony rolled into them.

She looked up just as Queen Isis's foot landed in the spot Chalcedony had just left.

Damn, that would have hurt. Compelling herself to remain steady, Chalcedony stood and pulled her sword from her waist, hoping the battle would be over before it started rejecting her.

"There is no weapon in existence that will help you against me."

"Go ahead. Pull yours out. I'll wait," Chalcedony lied. This was not an even fight. She needed every advantage she could get.

"I don't need a sword." Queen Isis lifted her arms. In an instant, her long, slender fingers changed into ten sharp talons. "I prefer to kill with my hands."

Chalcedony could change shape, but not instantly, and when she did it took hours of practice for her to resemble anything normal and not misshapen. Queen Isis made it seem as natural as breathing.

"You look scared," Queen Isis said.

I am. Chalcedony tightened the grip on her sword and embraced her fear. She may not be as powerful as Queen Isis, but she wielded a sword like no other. Talons? Hmph … what were talons compared to steel?

Queen Isis had disappeared and reappeared so quickly that Chalcedony hadn't known she was gone. One moment Queen Isis was in front of her and the next, she was behind.

Then, in a flash of light, they were no longer at the festival, but at the battlefield on the border of Queen Isis's land.

Chalcedony had grossly underestimated Queen Isis. She was now both fearful and envious of the queen. Had her mother possessed such power, speed, and strength? *Will I be this powerful after my coronation?*

Queen Isis hissed. "Tell your soldiers to retreat."

Chalcedony examined the battleground. It reeked of sweat, dirt, fear, and exhilaration. She heard the clamor of feet against the ground and the sharp clang of metal against metal. Her soldiers were told not to be heroes. But there were more than a few of them bloodied and motionless on the ground.

Queen Isis had reason to be concerned. She'd outnumbered Chalcedony's soldiers, but Chalcedony's soldiers were all fey and twice as deadly as a human. To make up for their lack of strength, the humans fought in pairs. But that hadn't been enough. There were more humans lying on the ground than fey. Chalcedony's army was winning.

Queen Isis's talons moved from Chalcedony's wrist to her bare neck. "Call them off."

"You're losing. Why should we retreat now?" Chalcedony's mood had lifted. She'd lost so many times over the past few days that she hadn't expected her army to be victorious. Queen Isis tightened her grip, cutting off Chalcedony's joy—and her air.

Just as she began to lose consciousness, Queen Isis loosened her grip just enough to let Chalcedony gasp for breath.

"I promised Coal that I wouldn't kill you," Queen Isis whispered, her breath hot on Chalcedony's ear. "But I will kill every one of your soldiers while you watch."

Chalcedony surveyed the organized chaos of the battlefield and understood the truth. Queen Isis could, and would, kill as many as necessary to get her way. Chalcedony nodded, and Queen Isis released her grip.

Chalcedony put her mother's sword back in its sheath. For a moment, she thought that Queen Isis would make her drop it. Instead, the queen stayed silent and followed Chalcedony as if she had no fear in the world.

One by one, the fighting stopped as the soldiers saw the queen and the princess together. They were bloodied, tired, and relieved. Royden jogged to the front of the struggle. *The bastard doesn't have a scratch on him. How is that possible?*

"Princess, is there something you want to say?" Royden asked with a wry smile, his hands resting on his sword. She scowled at him. Then something—someone—appeared beyond the fighting near her soldiers' tents. Tetrick. She suppressed a grin. There was a way out of this after all.

Chalcedony stood in front of her soldiers while she tried to think of something encouraging to say about their retreat, but she couldn't think of anything. They knew the plan. There was no point in making a big show of losing in front of Queen Isis.

She called to her fey. "Let's go home."

She stalked through the crowd, ignoring the look of confusion from Queen Isis's soldiers and the smug sense of triumph emanating from Royden. As she neared her tent, she felt a pleasurable sense of déjà vu.

CHAPTER TWENTY

Queen Isis's land had been cold, but it was beyond freezing in the human realm. Snow covered the ground, and the wind felt like ice against his skin.

"Where are we?" Lizzy asked, shivering. "Is my house near here?"

Coal turned in a circle, looking for something familiar. They were no longer on a treeless hill but in a forest full of evergreen trees. It was getting dark. The receding sun reflected off the surface of the snow, providing enough light to see.

"I don't think so. I don't know where we are," Coal admitted. When he'd come through the human realm with Chalcedony, there hadn't been any evergreen trees. The air didn't smell as clean as the fey realm, but it was better than the first time he'd gone to the human realm.

He wanted to ask for help, but he didn't know whom to trust. Queen Isis had warned him to be wary of Chalcedony's soldiers, but if anyone here were working for her, he couldn't tell who they were. He repositioned his coat, made sure Elizabeth was covered, and left the door.

"Where are we going?" Elizabeth asked. The snow was deep and soft. With every step, her foot sank into the powder. She grunted—from effort or annoyance Coal couldn't tell—whenever she pulled her foot out.

He stopped. "Let me carry you."

"No." She pulled away. "I'm not a baby. I can do it myself."

The fey that had come through the door with them were quickly dispersing. "We need to hurry. Everyone is leaving."

"I am," Elizabeth said with a sharp tone. "Do you even know how to get to my house?"

No. "Let's follow everyone else. Maybe we'll see something familiar."

She pulled her feet through the snow and grunted. Slowly, they trekked through the white forest. After half a mile, the forest ended, and they were standing near a wet, glistening road with a dozen different cars parked along it.

As they watched, two dwarves embraced before they stepped into a red car and drove away.

"We need a ride." Coal watched as more cars departed. A human stood against a truck. In the back sat two giants, an elf, and three dwarves. It looked crowded, but with a little bit of maneuvering, he and Elizabeth should be able to fit. And, more importantly, the driver was human, so the chances that he was helping Chalcedony were remote. As they approached, the man put something into his pocket and started to walk away.

"Excuse me," Coal said.

"I'm full," he said without looking in their direction.

"Where are we?" Coal asked.

Ignoring them, the man kept walking.

"Are we in Boston?" Elizabeth asked loudly. "I live in Boston, 777 Oakwood St, Boston, Massachusetts."

That got the man's attention. He stopped and eyed Elizabeth for a long moment. "You're in Ireland, lass."

So the door didn't only move, it also opened in different places. No one had bothered to tell him that.

"Can you help us get to Boston?" Coal asked.

"You human?" His face was red from the cold, and wrinkles branched out from the corners of his eyes.

"Yes," Coal and Elizabeth answered together. "We're human."

"And I'm trying to get home," Elizabeth continued.

"Take your hoods off and let me see."

They removed their hoods.

"Well, I'll be damned." He rubbed his thick brown beard. "What are two human kids doing in the middle of this mess?"

"We're trying to get to Boston," Coal said.

"I can't get you to Boston, but I can get you out of here and to the city. I'm sure someone in the government can help get you to America from there."

Elizabeth smiled and bounced from foot to foot.

"The back of my truck is full," the man continued, "but you can sit up front with me if you can pay for it."

"Uh …" Coal made a show of searching his pockets, knowing they were empty.

"Crossed over into the human realm without money, eh?" The way the man studied Coal made his stomach tighten. "Well," he said, "how about giving me that sword you have strapped to your back and I'll consider it even."

"No. This isn't mine," Coal said.

He walked away. "Nothing I can do for you then."

"Please don't leave us." Elizabeth ran after him. "I have a dagger."

He stopped, and Elizabeth showed him the weapon that Haline had given her.

"I can get a dozen of these for a dollar in the city. I want the sword." He motioned to Coal.

Coal looked up and down the road. More than half of the cars had left.

"It's cold. When are we getting out of here?" an elf from the back of the truck shouted.

"You heard 'em. I can't stand here bartering with you all night. If you want a ride, give me the sword."

"Please, Coal." Elizabeth clasped her hands together as if she were praying. "Please. My daddy will buy you a new one. I promise."

He'd promised himself that he'd bring Mischief back when he returned to the fey realm. What more would he have to give up? Slowly, Coal lifted the sword and its sheath from his back and gave it to the man. He smiled so brightly it seemed to light up the entire road.

"My name is Michael. It's been a pleasure doing business with you." He took the sword from its sheath before he grunted and dropped the weapon into its casing. "It burned me." Michael shook his hand.

"It's sentient, but it hasn't been bonded yet. So it chooses who wields it."

"Really?" Michael said with amazement. "I've heard stories about swords like this. I thought they were myths."

"I don't think it will let you use it. Perhaps you should give it back before it hurts you." Coal reached for Mischief, but Michael pulled it back.

"Don't worry. I'm going to put this darling above my fireplace. I won't need to use it."

The sword is meant to be used, not displayed, Coal thought.

Elizabeth climbed into the truck first. With a weariness that was more than physical, Coal followed. The seat squeaked as he sat, and the truck smelled of overly ripe strawberries. Michael opened the driver's side door and put the sword on the dashboard behind a small female figurine that shook its hips when Michael climbed in.

Michael lowered his window and shouted. "Welcome to the Fairyland Express. Is everybody ready to get the hell out of here?"

"Yes!" bellowed the voices from the back of the truck.

"Good. Let's go." Michael raised the window and started the truck. He drove a few yards before he turned the truck sharply. Elizabeth fell towards Coal, smashing him into the door. By the time they were upright again, the truck was facing the opposite direction.

"Oops, sorry about that!" Michael yelled. There were some grunts and a few nervous laughs from the back.

"We'll be in Dublin in no time. Two, three hours at the most," Michael said.

As they rode, snippets of conversation from the back leaked to the front. The fey were discussing what they were going to do when they got to the city. Some were going to stay in Dublin. Others were traveling to America, France, Johannesburg, Brazil—places Coal had only read about.

Coal closed his eyes and let the slight rocking of the truck relax him. Just as he was about to drift to sleep, he felt the truck slow before it stopped altogether.

"Are we there already?" Elizabeth asked.

"No, there's something in the road," Michael said.

Coal opened his eyes. Someone was standing in the middle of the road.

"What the hell?" Michael muttered before he lowered his window and shouted, "Get out of the damn road!"

The truck squeaked as the fey in the back moved.

"I am Princess Chalcedony," said a voice outside the truck.

"It's a damn fairy," Michael said under his breath. "There are no princesses in this country!" he yelled.

Of course, she wasn't going to make this easy. "I need my sword," Coal told Michael. "She's here for us."

"Well, this isn't fairyland. Princess or not, this is a democratic society. She can't come here and order people around." Michael reached underneath his seat and took out a long, cylindrical metallic object.

"Is that a gun?" Coal asked. Guns were not allowed in the fey realm, but there was a gun encased in the library at Legacy. Coal had always thought it seemed too little to do much damage, but what Michael held looked ominous.

"No, this is a rifle, but they both work the same." Michael stepped out of the truck. He approached Chalcedony with an arrogant swagger.

Coal didn't hear what they were saying, but it could not have been pleasant because Michael lifted his rifle. Before he was able to get the gun level, Chalcedony grabbed it and kicked his legs from underneath him. With her foot on his chest, she threw his weapon into the forest.

Elizabeth gasped just as Chalcedony glanced towards the truck.

"Come out, Coal and Elizabeth!" she shouted.

Coal sighed deeply, trying to control his anxiety. "Stay here," he told Elizabeth.

"Coal, can you drive? Maybe we can drive away," Elizabeth said.

"No, Lizzy. It's okay. I'll think of something."

She nodded while he grabbed Mischief from the dashboard.

CHAPTER TWENTY-ONE

Coal stepped out of the truck and walked slowly towards Chalcedony and Michael. With Mischief strapped to his back, he hoped he appeared more confident than he felt. The snow was falling faster, and it was starting to blanket the road. His hands were both sweaty and cold. Sooner than he'd expected, he stood across from Chalcedony. Michael struggled with renewed urgency.

Her new pale skin revealed large purple and blue bruises on her neck. Her right eye was bloodshot. She looked terrible, but none of that registered in her stance. How had she escaped Queen Isis? Had she defeated a full queen?

Chalcedony kept her foot on Michael's chest.

"You can let him go now. I'm here," Coal said.

Chalcedony removed her foot and Michael stood up. He was about to run towards his truck, but Chalcedony grabbed his wrist and pulled him back. "Go get the girl and bring her to me," she told him.

"She isn't an elf. You have no business here," Michael said.

Chalcedony tightened her grip on his wrist.

"Okay. Okay," he said through his pain. "I'll get her. I'll get her."

She released him and he walked away, cursing.

"How did you get here so quickly? I just saw you and Queen Isis disappear," Coal asked, trying to keep his voice from shaking.

"I asked for help." Chalcedony motioned towards the dark forest.

Who, Coal wondered, *could get her here so quickly?* Tetrick. Only queens and sometimes their children had the ability to phase through the two realms. "You've always hated asking for help."

"Well, I've learned a lot over the past few days." Chalcedony stepped towards Coal. "I let Queen Isis and Royden think they'd defeated me and that I was on my way home. She may be stronger than me, but she isn't smarter. Are you ready to go?"

He couldn't let it end this way. "I'm not going back with you. Not yet. Not until I get Lizzy home."

"You don't have a choice. This time there is no one here to rescue you. There are no crazy dwarves, no rogue human shadows, no wild dragons, and no insane queens. You cannot defeat me on your own."

"How about I fight you for it? If I win, you let me take Lizzy home. If you win, we'll come back with you without a fight."

"You've already lost," Chalcedony said.

"What do you have to lose? I've never been able to beat you."

Before Chalcedony answered, Michael returned with Elizabeth. He met Coal's gaze and shifted his shoulders in an apology. With a nod, Coal tried to tell the man he understood.

Chalcedony needed to hurry, get Coal and Elizabeth, and get out of this realm, but phasing was hard enough with just one person. Tetrick needed Coal and Elizabeth to come willingly or they wouldn't make it to where they needed to be. "Again, why would I accept a challenge from you?" Chalcedony didn't want Coal to know she needed him to come without a fight.

Coal bit his lip. The hood of his coat covered most of his face, but his large eyes and thick eyelashes were hard to hide. Through them, she saw his mind racing for a way out of this. She reached for his arm.

"Let's go, Coal."

"No." He stepped back, almost falling onto the ground. "Queen Isis and Royden offered to make me a prince. If you win, I'll return to Legacy and accept my punishment. When they come for me, I'll tell Queen Isis that Elizabeth and I are with you willingly."

"Queen Isis can't make you a prince." Chalcedony stepped towards Coal once again. "You're a human."

Coal pulled out Mischief and pointed it at her. "Queen Isis has a human lover, and she lets fey and humans travel through her door freely. She does whatever she wants."

Chalcedony's face and neck ached as she recalled the beating the queen had given her. Queen Isis would probably come for them, especially if Coal had told the truth about the offer to become a prince. Chalcedony looked forward to fighting Queen Isis when she was more experienced. Until then, she needed time to train and prepare.

"You know you can't win, Coal."

"I just need to try." Coal removed his hood and lifted her stolen sword higher.

Coal was right. The longer she delayed, the more likely Queen Isis or Royden would notice and come looking for Coal. "Both of you need to promise you'll come with me after I win."

He regarded Elizabeth and then Chalcedony. "If you win, I promise."

"Lizzy needs to promise also," Chalcedony said.

"Elizabeth, promise Chalcedony you'll come."

"But Coal—" Elizabeth began.

"Just promise."

"I promise," Elizabeth mumbled and averted her eyes.

Chalcedony glanced from the girl and then to the trees where Tetrick waited. She couldn't see him, but she knew he was watching. She felt as if she was in a training session in the human realm and this was her final test.

She pulled out Mayhem. It hadn't fully accepted her yet, but Chalcedony was wielding it as well as she believed her mother would have. Defeating him would be quick and easy, and she knew she could do it before Mayhem turned on her.

Elizabeth, Michael, and the fey from the back of the truck watched a few feet away. But as Coal stood with his weapon ready across from Chalcedony, it felt like they were the only living things left in the world.

Despite the lack of sunlight, Mayhem's steel gleamed, emitting a light all its own.

"Let's get this over with," she said. "The first to draw blood wins."

His hand ached from the dragon fight and he needed to warm up. However, Chalcedony didn't need time to prepare. She rushed towards him, her sword aiming for Coal's neck. He didn't have enough time to meet the blow, so he jumped back and out of the way, tripping over a rock and landing hard on his ass.

Coal jumped to his feet, gripping his sword and thankful that he hadn't dropped it.

Chalcedony grinned while she stood across from him. She could have ended it while he was on his back, but she hadn't. It should have been a relief; instead it made him feel like he was being toyed with.

Controlling his growing fear and shaking away the snow that clung to his back, he stepped forward and took the offensive. The ringing sound of metal against metal reverberated down the road and the surrounding forest as they fought.

After Coal's strongest attack, Chalcedony clenched her jaw, and with three consecutive overhand strikes, she forced Coal to lose the little bit of ground he had gained.

In spite of the cold, he perspired. His hand throbbed, and he feared he'd drop his weapon. It was as if he'd forgotten everything he'd learned from Grigory.

His sword knew they were losing and it pulsed with displeasure. He didn't know how he was going to beat Chalcedony, but if he panicked, he'd never be able to figure it out.

Chalcedony attacked so fast he barely registered her movements until they ended. Out of instinct more than any defensive strategy, he was able to avoid her blows.

"What's wrong, Coal?" Her lips were twisted into a cocky grin.

"You've been toying with me all these years, pretending you were weaker than you were," he said, realizing the truth; he was no match for her.

She shrugged. "If I'm not the strongest person in my land, I will be once I am coroneted. Did you really think you had a chance?"

"Why did you make me believe I almost beat you the last time we fought?" Coal asked.

"Madoc Rule Number Seven: Never Let Anyone Know Your True Strength Until You Absolutely Have To." Her face glistened from melted snow. "Not even your best friend."

Three days ago, that would have hurt, a week ago it would have kept him up at night, but she'd just repeated something she'd already taught him. She had never trusted him, and he had been naive to have trusted her. Burying his hurt feelings and broken heart, his mind raced as he tried to think of a way out of this before Chalcedony decided to attack again. He didn't have Djamel's speed or Cesaro's strength. He couldn't change his fingers into talons like Queen Isis. But Haline didn't have any exceptional powers. She wasn't exceptionally strong and she hardly used a sword. When he first met her, she had used speed and force to take him down.

Knowing he couldn't win with his sword, he threw it with all the strength left in his arms. His hunch paid off, Chalcedony's gaze followed Mischief as it disappeared in the darkness of the forest. While she was distracted, he sprinted towards her as fast as he could. She looked back just as Coal collided into her. He grabbed on to her waist and her sword fell from her hand as they both hit the ground. From the sound of Chalcedony's head hitting the pavement, Coal knew she must be in pain, but she didn't skip a beat. As soon as she hit the ground, she tried to roll over, but he held her waist with all of his strength. The awkward position prevented her from moving easily. He didn't know what he was going to do next, but at least she didn't have a sword anymore.

Coal was so intent on holding on to her and thinking of his next move that he didn't notice when she stopped moving. Chalcedony's sword moved towards her. She was using magic. Damn, he had forgotten she could do that. Before he could grab her, she already had the sword in her hand.

He released her and jumped away.

She stood, her chest heaving from exertion. "That was a dirty trick, Coal." She removed a hand from her sword and touched the back of her head. She pulled it away covered in blood.

"You're bleeding," Coal said.

With disbelief in her eyes, she quickly gripped the sword again as if she were trying to hide the blood.

"You're bleeding. You lose." The realization that he had drawn first blood occurred to him and ignited a fountain of hope.

"No," Chalcedony scowled. "This is a sword fight. You didn't use a sword." The snow fell heavier and her hair was quickly covered with it. Already some of it had melted and dripped onto the ground.

"You're bleeding. I won," Coal declared.

"You didn't win. You cheated."

"That wasn't cheating," Coal said, with more confidence than he felt. "You told me no good fighter only uses a sword. I won. Now, keep your word and let us leave."

She sneered. "You are going to have to kill me first, and we both know you don't have the strength or the courage for that."

She stepped towards Coal, but one of the male giants who had been sitting in the back of the truck stepped between the two of them. "It's over. You lost." The giant towered over Chalcedony by two and a half feet.

Chalcedony reared back and raised her sword. "I'll cut you both down if I have to."

"It's over, Princess." A dwarf spoke this time, his voice deep and threatening. "You can't take us all out." Then others from the back of the truck stepped up.

Her sword stayed steady as she pointed the sword down the row. "Do you understand what you are doing? I will be queen."

"If you were a queen you'd be able to take us all out, but you're not," the giant said. "So leave."

"You think you won, don't you?" She laughed so hard she bent over and held her belly, her sword still held awkwardly in her hand.

The sound was an odd mixture of insanity and joy. "You're returning to a world that threw you away. The human realm is filthy. Yes, congratulations. You won. You'll never see me or the fey realm again." She sheathed her sword and strolled confidently into the forest.

She only said those things to shake his confidence and make losing easier for her. He'd done the right thing and now Elizabeth was headed home to her parents. But maybe she had been right. What had he won?

"Are you okay?" Elizabeth asked, drawing Coal's attention. Was he?

He forced a smile as he placed the sword back into its sheath. "Yeah, I'm fine. Are you ready to go home?"

Elizabeth nodded. She'd taken off her hood, and her dark hair spilled onto the back of her coat, her cheeks red from the cold.

"You showed her," said the female giant with light skin and straight short hair. "That bitch got what she deserved."

"I wouldn't be so happy if I was you," the giant's male companion said. "The queenling, unlike Queen Isis, patrols the human realm for rogue fey. Now we're going to have to watch our back for the entire time we're here."

"Ireland is under Queen Isis's protection, not Princess Chalcedony's," the dwarf said. He had a heart-shaped face with long wavy black hair. He didn't wear a coat and his jaw shivered as he spoke.

"Tell that to the weavers once she captures you."

"Regardless, standing here waiting for her to come back isn't going to do any good. Let's get the hell out of here," Michael said.

"Do you really think she'll come back for us?" Elizabeth asked once they were in the truck.

"No," Coal said. "She never wants to see me again, and I'm sure that includes you, too."

The End

Book 2 of the Everleaf Series

"Wake up, boy."

Coal opened his eyes. A short, heavily muscled human with a gold tooth and a tight gray uniform stood above him. His badge read: D. Abraham.

"Get up. Someone wants to meet you."

Coal stood, put on his slippers that were only slightly less hard than the floor, and let the guard restrain his hands and feet. He knew not to ask questions.

He'd grown half a foot in the past three months, and he towered above the guards and most people here.

When he'd first arrived at what he learned were detention centers, people were scared of him. Well, they were scared of him until he talked and they realized he was young and naive, and his accent told people he was different, and different was not good in this place.

After a few fights, he'd learned to stay quiet. The less people knew about you, the more they were scared.

D. Abraham led him past another guard standing outside of the cell. They were always in pairs. As they escorted him down the gray hall, he felt the gaze of the other inmates. If he'd learned anything over the past three months, it was to never show fear. He stood straighter and sneered as he passed the boy he'd fought with yesterday.

The guards stopped at a room a few floors beneath his cell.

A man with a blue suit stood as Coal entered the room. "I'm Agent Ellis." He extended his hand for Coal to shake.

Coal nodded and sat down. Don't shake someone's hand if you don't trust them. Since he'd been in the human realm, he'd learned not to trust anyone, especially the people he met in these small rooms.

Mr. Ellis continued to stand. "Coal, right?"

He stayed silent.

"Ah." The man sat down. "I get it. You're all jaded now. You're not talking anymore." He paused, looking expectantly towards Coal, and then he began again. "You're mad because you've been thrown in jail, and you feel like you've been mistreated. Well, answer this. How should you be treated? You were an accessory to kidnapping. The mother felt so guilty over the abduction of her child that she killed herself. So, I repeat, how should you be treated?"

"I brought her back." Coal bit back guilt and regret. He'd done all he could to get Elizabeth home. In the end, he'd succeeded. It just hadn't been soon enough.

ABOUT THE AUTHOR

Constance Burris is on a journey to take over the world by writing fantasy, horror, and science fiction. Her mission is to spread the love of speculative fiction to the masses. She is a proud card carrying blerd (black nerd), mother, and wife. When she is not writing and spending time with her family, she is working hard as an environmental engineer in Oklahoma City.

www.twitter.com/constanceburris
www.facebook.com/constance.burris
www.constanceburris.com

AUTHOR NOTES

Please help me on my mission to take over the world, and leave a review on Goodreads, Amazon, Smashwords, and/or Barnes and Noble. World domination is impossible without ~~helpful minions, subjects, faithful followers~~ book reviews.

I absolutely love to talk to readers, so please connect with me through Facebook, Google+, Twitter, or my blog. I really want to know how you feel about Chalcedony. Good girl gone bad, or is she just misunderstood? Personally, I feel like she's misunderstood, but I have a soft spot for bad girls.

Calling all artists! If you are suddenly overtaken by the desire to make *Coal* character sketches, send them to me and I'll showcase them on my blog, Pinterest, and Tumblr and credit you.

Don't Forget…Stay in the know and subscribe to my mailing list, where I'll be sending progress reports about the second book and other future releases.

ALSO BY CONSTANCE BURRIS

BLACK BEAUTY

Shemeya knocked on Jason's door. For the past two years, they'd ended up in the same chemistry course as lab partners. He'd asked her out a few times but she'd politely said no. He bored her. Turning him down made her feel like an idiot who only went out with thugs, but she wasn't stupid. She only wanted a little thug, not a full serving.

When Jason opened the door, she pulled off her backpack and stepped into his house. "Is your mom home?"

"No, she's with her new guy." He led her into his kitchen. "Want something to drink?"

"You got some juice?" She desperately wanted to get rid of the dry, earthy taste that the herbs had left in her mouth. Water hadn't worked.

"I got something better." He reached under one of the kitchen cabinets and pulled out a bottle of Hennessy.

"Jason, really?"

He smiled innocently.

She rolled her eyes. "Sure. I need a drink after the day I've had." *And liquor should kill the taste in my mouth.*

He poured the cognac into two yellow plastic cups, before they walked into the living room and sat on his couch. The alcohol warmed her insides and seared away the taste of the herbs.

"We should be talking about absorption, not sitting here getting drunk," Shemeya pointed out.

"We always finish our projects tipsy. Why should this time be any different?"

Shemeya laughed. "Anyways, let's get started: absorption vs. adsorption." She pulled her chemistry book from her backpack.

"Stupid names. Why do they have to be so similar?" He sat back on the couch with a glazed look in his eyes.

"Are you going to get your books?"

He licked his lips and leaned forward. "I've heard stories about you and Latreece's boyfriend."

"So?" The buzz she had from the liquor quickly dissipated while her heart rate increased. She dreaded where the conversation was headed.

"I don't understand. I've been asking you out for months, but you go out with him instead. He has a girlfriend."

"I didn't go out with him," she said through clenched teeth. She'd expected to be harassed at school; she hadn't expected it here. She had hoped her anger would shut him up, but no such luck.

"I saw you go in the room with Corey last weekend at Serena's party."

She threw her books on the table and stood. "Oh damn, Jason. Really?"

"I've treated you with nothing but respect since I've known you."

"I've had a horrible day with everyone teasing me at school. Now I get here and have to deal with it from you, too. I'm leaving." She turned from him and bent over to pick up her books.

"Are you crying?"

She brought her hand up to her face and it came back wet. Why was she crying in front of him? Wasn't the fake weed supposed to give her courage?

"Don't go. I'm sorry."

She was so busy wiping away her tears that she didn't fight it when he grabbed her hand and pulled her back onto the couch. "I'm sorry. I shouldn't have said anything."

She let him hold her as she cried. Maybe it was the liquor, maybe it was the fake weed, or maybe it was her loneliness, but whatever the reason, she didn't stop him when he brought his lips down onto hers.

His sweaty hands on her breast brought her back to reality. He wasn't who she wanted. "No, Jason." She pulled back. "I have to go."

"Don't go," he pleaded, with his hand still under her shirt. Somehow they'd ended up on the couch with him on top cradled between her legs.

"No." She tried to move from under him.

He loomed above her, flushed despite his dark skin. "Do you like it rough? Is that what it is?"

"No. This isn't what I came here for." Shemeya tore at his chest, but Jason refused to budge.

He kissed her neck. "I'm tired of being the nice guy," he murmured, pinning her further beneath his body.

"Get off me!" she screamed. His erection rubbed against the crotch of her jeans. She punched and kicked, but it made him more excited. Her scalp itched as she fought. She wanted to scratch, but she needed both hands to fight Jason off. *I'm getting raped, but I can't fight the urge to scratch.* The inconvenience of it almost made her laugh.

Something above moved. She looked past Jason. Five snakes were hovering above his head.

"I'm going crazy." This time she did laugh, and the snakes, which were the same rusty brown color as her dreads, smiled.

Jason looked towards her. "Why are you laughing?" His eyes darted above her. The feel of his erection disappeared as he crept away, but she wrapped her legs around his waist.

Her itching scalp had been replaced with pleasurable tingles that ran from her head down to her toes. "Where are you going?" she asked.

"We need to leave," he said, trembling. "There are snakes in here. There are snakes in your hair." She pulled him closer while he fought to be released. "Let go. We need to get out of here."

"No, stay," she whispered in his ear. "They won't hurt you."

Shaking, he looked from Shemeya to the snakes. He tried to force himself from her legs. This time, when she tried to pull him closer, he punched her. Pain exploded in her jaw, but she never let go.

"Jason, that hurt."

He looked into her eyes. "Please," he begged. A snake sunk its fangs into his cheek. Another struck his ear. One clung to his nose, and another hung below his left eye. He writhed in pain as he tried to escape the snakes and her thighs. His pleading eyes came back to her before he stopped moving completely. The snakes retracted their fangs. She relaxed her legs. Jason fell onto the carpeted floor.

She stood and nearly fainted before she righted herself by grabbing the side of the couch. She brought her hands up to fix her hair, but hesitated a few inches away. She'd never touched snakes before. But the snakes came to her, caressing her open palm. They were cold and smooth and full of life.

The Complete Black Beauty series coming September 2015

Printed in Great Britain
by Amazon

59469117R00130